When Water Wants To

When Water Wants To

The DALRO Can Themba Merit Award Short Story Anthology

EDITED BY NEIL COPPEN

Published in South Africa by:

Wits University Press
1 Jan Smuts Avenue
Johannesburg
www.witspress.co.za

First published 2025

http://dx.doi.org.10.18772/22025109797

978-1-77614-979-7 (Paperback)
978-1-77614-980-3 (Hardback)
978-1-77614-981-0 (Web PDF)
978-1-77614-982-7 (EPUB)

This publication is part of a collaborative project with:

Project manager: Alison Paulin
Copyeditor: Tuelo Gabonewe
Proofreader: Inga Norenius
Cover design: Triple M
Typeset in 12 point Caslon Pro

CONTENTS

PREFACE

Anthologies of short stories are able to offer us fascinating peeks into the collective consciousness of a country and its creative thinkers. The title of this collection, *When Water Wants To*, alludes to a certain mercurial element that readers may notice – trickling, weaving, eddying, murmuring, flowing and weeping across the course of the ten stories included in this publication.

Water can be found withheld in the communal taps of an informal settlement in Dyondzo Kwinika's 'Mr Duiker Sang the Blues', the changing hues in a haunted swimming pool in Jacqui Aires' 'No Good Deed', or present in the mischievous Atlantic tides that mar a seaside picnic in Rosieda Shabodien's 'The Watermelon Caretaker'.

Water provides the endangered habitat of the mythological (not to mention corruptible) mermaid queen featured in Lerato Mahlangu's 'Zombie' while also forming a part of the hallucinatory bathing rituals that her protagonist Wanda is forced to participate in.

In the poetic closing passages of Sebabatso Madibu's 'Letters of Remembrance' it's recalled in the form of healing raindrops that bend the spinach leaves, and it features in Princess Unarine Rabada's 'The Woman Who Buried Rain' as both restorative thundershowers and tears stored in a precious clay gourd to mark the period of grief endured by the story's protagonist Munei.

Before diving further into some of the themes and concerns that span this collection, allow me to offer a little context into how this project and publication came into being. In early 2025, The DALRO Can Themba Merit Award launched an open call for South African writers to submit authentic and engaging short stories, stories which sought – in the spirit of the eponymous writer – to provide nuanced literary glimpses into South African life.

The competition was created to offer a platform for emerging writers while at the same time setting out to celebrate the legacy of one of South Africa's literary giants, Can Themba.

Themba launched his career by writing for *Drum* magazine in the 1950s where he published a range of articles drawing attention to both the brutalities and the absurdities of life under apartheid. These social critiques and anecdotal accounts, set in Johannesburg townships, would often coalesce into powerful works of short fiction, including one of the author's most beloved and enduring stories, *The Suit*.

For those who have not yet acquainted themselves with this Sophiatown-set classic, *The Suit* follows a man named Philemon who, after learning about his wife Matilda's infidelity, sets about exacting a humiliating revenge on her. First published in 1963, Themba's *The Suit* continues to reach new audiences partly due to the successes of the many theatrical adaptations that have occurred since its publication.

These adaptations include those by Mothobi Mutloatse and Barney Simon at the Market Theatre in 1994, and Peter Brook, whose French translation *Le Costume* premiered at the Théâtre des Bouffes du Nord in Paris in 1999. More recently, dramatists have begun to search elsewhere in Themba's canon, unearthing dramatic potential in stories such as *Crepuscule* which was successfully adapted for the stage by my friend Khayelihle Dom Gumede in 2012.

The DALRO Can Themba Merit Award looks to expand on the potential of such cross-disciplinary/pollinatory creativity, seeking entries that, like many of Themba's stories, stand alone as powerful literary works while at the same time containing seeds of characters and scenarios that might be ripe for dramatic reinterpretation on the stage.

It's for this reason that this competition spans a two-year developmental cycle with the first component culminating in the pages of this very anthology. For this part of the process, a panel was drawn from South African literary and dramatic circles and included myself working alongside Tiisetso Mashifane, Niq Mhlongo, Lorraine Sithole, Lynn Joffe, Greg Homann and Shafinaaz Hassim.

Together we were tasked with deliberating over two hundred entries in order to arrive at a top ten. After the winners were announced, a mentorship process began whereby I supported and guided the writers in further crafting and refining their stories.

The second phase of the project will see one of the ten writers included in this book (not yet announced at the time of going to print) chosen to further adapt and develop their story into a stage play that will premiere at The Market Theatre in 2026.

These dual outcomes, while exciting to consider, have caused occasional deliberations (albeit generative ones) in the judging process. The short story and the play remain two very different disciplines. What makes for a memorable short work of fiction/non-fiction does not always contain the necessary ingredients to cook up a thrilling new play. As judges we debated questions such as: Does one discount a well-written short story based on its lack of potential to exist as a full-length play, and what about those submissions that contained rich possibilities for theatrical adaptation but didn't quite work when condensed into the short story format?

A short story is, after all, a tricky literary form to master. With word counts that prohibit reams of exposition and backstory, every character, sentence, word, description and plot meander must be whittled down to its most essential parts. Writers of the short story are forced to develop a ruthless sense of economy in the telling of their tales. It's this brevity that makes a short story so frustrating to write but thrilling to read. There's none of the elaborate and gradual world-building afforded to the novelist. Instead, we cut directly to the chase, are transposed to the epicentre of it all, often encountering characters suspended in a limbo, poised at a crossroads, soliloquising over a pivotal decision that needs to be made and inevitably longing for a resolution or closure of some sort.

One of the most useful questions I've kept posing to the writers featured in this publication is why choose *this* particular day in your character's life to locate your story within? What is it about this moment, this day – over the millions of others that constitute your character's life story – that is able to offer readers a critical insight that their last month, yesterday or tomorrow couldn't quite match?

Can Themba starts his story *The Suit* with little preamble. We meet the characters on the same morning on which Philemon is tipped off about his wife Matilda's infidelity and returns home from work to have his worst fears confirmed. Sure enough, Philemon witnesses a man – clad in a vest and underpants – fleeing down the street, his blue suit remaining behind. This suit is wielded by Philemon as a cruel prop and used for the remainder of the story to torment and humiliate Matilda.

It's a simple but effective premise that, once established, propels the story forward with an urgent momentum over its brief but powerful eight-page duration.

Perhaps this is why short stories, like Themba's, often go on to inspire successful theatrical adaptations. Theatre, like the short story, is mostly driven by a conceit or premise that lands characters in some sort of dramatic action early on in the telling. Playwriting – like the short story – does not share the same expansive story-telling toolkit afforded to that of the novelist or screenwriter. Time in both the short story and play is often condensed and with this, the dramatic stakes are heightened.

Similarly, when it comes to adapting a novel for the stage, the playwright is left with the task of distilling reams of story down to its essential core, whereas the short story offers far more room for collaborative re-imagining.

All of this brings us to the collection of new South African writing compiled in this anthology. As volume editor on the project, it's been fascinating to see the unexpected correlations and conversations these stories – dreamed up from opposite ends of the country – are able to now have with one another. It's like arriving at a dinner party and sitting down to share a meal with ten unknown but deeply compelling strangers.

In the competition call, no single theme or topic was specified and so submissions ranged from deeply personal autobiographical accounts to some bold genre experiments with horror and science fiction. Submissions were made by writers from different generations, cultures and provinces. For a majority of the top ten, these submissions constituted their first attempt at short story writing.

What interested the panel, beyond the deliberations I have mentioned earlier about short story–play adaptability, was how the writers' stories spoke to contemporary realities. South African writers have often preoccupied themselves with disentangling a traumatic past, but how are newer generations of storytellers writing about and making sense of our equally complex present?

Stories seldom take place in a vacuum and what unites many of these narratives is the way in which provinces, towns, cities and suburbs from across the country feature almost as characters in themselves.

Over the course of this anthology, readers will travel the length and breadth of the country including a visit to the Vhembe District of Limpopo, a province that borders Botswana, Zimbabwe and Mozambique. It's in the drought-stricken village of Dzimauli where Princess Unarine Rabada's story 'The Woman Who Buried Rain' is set, and it's under the shades of the marula tree where we first meet Munei, a woman grieving the loss of her husband and son. Throughout this fable, Rabada treats us to a moving and magical meditation on love and grief and writes in a style that recalls the allegorical whimsy of South African national treasure Mam' Gcina Mhlophe.

In Lerato Mahlangu's irreverent take on the horror genre, 'Zombie', we are quite literally swept up with her protagonist Wanda by a whirlwind that rips through the dusty soccer fields and gated communities of Duvha Park in Witbank, Mpumalanga. It's this inciting incident that comes with some pretty dire supernatural repercussions when Wanda realises that in the storm's aftermath, he has been reduced to a gormless, leering zombie, a creature whose nightly exploits further colour our understanding of his community and neighbour-hood. 'I am a zombie, reincarnated, so I must do zombie things,' Wanda explains.

> I walk from the Lynnville Mortuary to a veld in Duvha Park where I rest and eat dry leaves. When the sun sets I walk to Modelpark into Riverbank Estate and fight my way past two strong guards who try to stop me from entering. The dogs growl when they see me walk by and I growl back, watching them cower.

What makes Mahlangu's 'Zombie' so refreshing is that it steers clear of the flesh-eating zombie tropes popula-rised by American horror films and roots the story in a uniquely South African cultural context of the zombie figuration. While the isiZulu concept of *ukuthwebula* may sound like a fantastical literary conceit to some, for many South Africans it's a very real form of witchcraft and sorcery whereby a person's soul is captured and controlled by another.

In Dyondzo Kwinika's 'Mr Duiker Sang the Blues', an informal settlement outside Daggafontein, Johannesburg, comes to shape the worldview of his weary protagonist. Bra Ebenezer, we are told, first arrived in the settlement as a refugee from war-torn Mozambique and over the course of his life has made many sacrifices, including turning to a life of crime, in an attempt to raise his own children out of poverty.

Much to Ebenezer's relief, his son Themba has managed to carve a name for himself as an award-winning musician, but beneath the acclaim and plaudits, Themba suffers from a crippling depression that no amount of paternal love, success or compassion can temper. Kwinika's unflinching descriptions of the social conditions in the settlement combined with the deep empathy with which he imbues each of his characters, I believe, pays homage to some of Can Themba's most memorable writing.

In a passage detailing Themba's childhood in the Daggafontein settlement, Ebenezer recalls:

He danced barefoot to Brenda Fassie's Nomakanjani, arms wide. Slipped between the shacks. No one saw him. Children loitered near the communal tap, waiting for water that came when it wanted. Not when it was needed. Wire cars swerved through garbage mounds. Sewage cut through dirt paths. Flies everywhere. Scuffles broke out. Pebbles scattered. Voices rose. Then *diketo* carried on, near the shack where we found him. He was under the table, cake on his face. Said he'd be famous one day. He was my boy. Their Brown Antelope.

In Sebabatso Madibu's 'Letters of Remembrance' we remain in Johannesburg but are cast into a dystopian reimagining of the city and its surrounds in the latter parts of the twenty-first century. The air has become too toxic to breathe and humans are assimilating with machines in order to survive the volatile changes in climate and political instabilities. The price to be paid for undergoing this procedure is that they must be prepared to surrender their memories in the process.

Madibu's story is relayed through a series of letters written by Nandipha to her ailing father, each documenting the phases of surgery where parts of her mind and body are augmented with new technologies.

Before I left.
You called it neural integration.

A surgical phase that bends the past out of shape.
So we forget the kind of joy they can't sell back to us.
We forget that the sun shines without asking for
  anything.
Laminating Berea in native light.
In Sandton, the sun doesn't shine like the one back
  home.
Instead it stares; without promise.
Like the mystery of existence.
'Please my child,' Mama said.
'Just go build a better life.'

Throughout *Letters*, Madibu urges the reader never to take for granted the precious acts and artefacts, rights and rituals that make us human. In exploring ideas of 'assimilation' through an Afrofuturist lens, we are asked to consider how much of one's community, culture, language and beliefs must be forfeited when one merges with the prevailing status quo.

The next province we visit is the Western Cape where Megan Choritz's *Murmur Becomes a Wave* casts a sardonic lens over the paranoiac shenanigans of largely white suburbia. Over a few tense pages, we witness how news of a snatched handbag and the presence of a man of colour wearing a hoodie and exercising in a park in a local suburb sets off a tsunami of rumours and misunderstandings which swiftly escalate into senseless tragedy.

Also set in Cape Town, Kamva Majo's 'A Mortician's Instinct' is a twisted love story that sees her mortician, Mandla, carrying out a mysterious organisation's commands while attempting to bury a terrible secret during the pandemic lockdowns.

Mandla's daily commute, moving between the township of Khayelitsha and the suburb of Mowbray, sees him straddle two opposing worlds. Although these communities lie relatively close together, in her story Majo depicts the dramatic spatial/class differences that characterise much of the South African experience.

> Mandla's Mortuary stood in Khayelitsha – twenty-five minutes from his home in Mowbray.
> He had grown up in Khayelitsha.
> The streets there knew the sound of mourning better than music.
> Death wasn't a tragedy there – it was routine. Quick. Expected.
> That's why he built his business there. Not because it was home, but because death felt normal there. But he moved to Mowbray, thinking he would be far away from it. In Mowbray, people watered their lawns. Smiled at strangers in the mornings. Pretended.
> Even their mourning appeared organised. Eyes dry. No women hurled to the floor by the weight of grief, wailing from the gut.

They stayed still – crumbling quietly behind closed doors.

A train carrying an excitable family along the shores of the False Bay coastline towards the fishing village of Kalk Bay is the premise behind Rosieda Shabodien's autobiographical 'The Watermelon Caretaker'. As the story unfolds, we are transported into the haunted history that is commonly rendered invisible within the beauty of these seaside sites of leisure and recreation. For many brown and black South Africans, the pain inflicted on them in the past during periods of forced removals and segregation lingers on and echoes in the present. Shabodien's bittersweet testimony keeps the complexity of family, memory and erasure in a delicate dance across the watery landscapes of South Africa's history.

As Shabodien recalls:

A narrow, winding serpentine road, just a few metres from the water's edge, winds its way along the base of the mountain. Beside it, a railway track mirrors every twist of the road's curves – two parallel conduits carrying tales of happiness and hardship. At the edge of the village, the fishing harbour bustles, alive with the sounds of clanging masts and colourful boats bobbing as fishermen haul in their catch or head out to sea. Seals slip in and out of the waves, scavenging for scraps, while seagulls shriek overhead, poised to snatch a piece of fish. It forms the final flourish in a picture-perfect postcard of a seaside village. Yet beneath that idyllic, charming façade, the tide still drags out a sorrowful tale.

A more literal haunting stalks the hapless new owners of a house in Jacqui Aires' 'No Good Deed'. Aires spins a satirical yarn probing the perils of home ownership in contemporary South Africa while evoking sites of forced removals like Triomf in Sophiatown and Zonnebloem in District Six. No matter what extremes the couple Phil and Tilda go to as they try to erase the traces of those who came before, any attempt to settle into their new home is met with an overwhelming supernatural resistance.

Aires' take on the haunted house narrative surfaces unsettling questions around what historic 'deeds' in South Africa remain unpunished. In the end, Phil and Tilda seem set to lose everything ... including what remains of their sanity.

Moving now to Ulundi, KwaZulu-Natal, the 'sanity' of Lethukukhanya Mzulwini's protagonist Thandaza in the story 'African Death, Western Medicine' is also very much called into question when we first meet her. Thandaza has recently returned from the psychiatric ward, unable to resolve the tensions that exist between her Christian faith and a calling she has received from her ancestors. Psychiatrists, Thandaza's patriarchal pastor husband and community members all offer opinions and advice to explain her many miscarriages and deteriorating mental health, but who should she believe? Are her increasing misfortunes the result of demon possession, grief, ancestral rage or schizophrenia? Caught in this tangle of opinion and diagnosis, Thandaza must arrive at a definitive choice about which spiritual path to pursue and which to turn her back on.

Dashalia Singaram's 'Man of the House: An Eldest Daughter's Story' is the second KwaZulu-Natal-set story featured in this anthology and follows a young woman named Seva, whose return to her childhood home in Pietermaritzburg to visit her estranged father awakens a complex series of memories and recollections. She recalls:

Pietermaritzburg had become renowned since I'd escaped at the age of eighteen. First came the Ubers. Then the riots. For many South Africans, that was the first time they heard of the town. And first impressions live long past the tragedy that follows. Before that, there were stories of cannibalism, political assassinations and serial killers. Femicide ran rampant through the suburbs and the settlements. Just down the road from my mother's house, a man once beat his girlfriend to death and cut off her head. Domestic disputes had evolved into domestic terrorism and I had the startling realisation that I, too, was in danger of contributing to those statistics.

In both 'Man of the House' and 'Mr Duiker Sang the Blues' we witness the dynamics of a father-daughter/son relationship relayed through first person narration. In 'Mr Duiker Sang the Blues' the story is told from the father Ebenezer's point of view, a man who despite his best attempts is unable to reverse his son's decision to take his own life, while in 'Man of the House' this perspective shifts to that of a daughter reflecting on her inability to rescue her father from the clutches of booze and nihilism.

Death, as with the healing and destructive forces of water I discussed earlier, seems to permeate each of the stories included in this anthology, whether it's in a father grappling with the assisted suicide of his son in 'Mr Duiker', the mortician's grim secret behind 'A Mortician's Instinct', the senseless killing of an innocent man in 'Murmur Becomes a Wave', the grisly homicide that underpins the present day ghost story in 'No Good Deed', or the stillbirths that haunt Thandaza in 'African Death, Western Medicine'. In both 'The Watermelon Caretaker' and 'Letters of Remembrance' the act of writing serves as a way to memorialise loved ones who have either passed on or are nearing the end of their lives. Then there's Wanda in 'Zombie', a man who is neither dead nor alive but hovers in the existential limbo of somewhere in between.

Death, of course, isn't a recent preoccupation for South African writers. Can Themba alongside his *Drum* colleagues famously lived by the adage: 'Live fast, die young and have a good-looking corpse'. Writing out in defiance of the apartheid regime naturally came with its own set of risks and Can Themba and his colleagues remained fearless in doing so. Yet to this day, even after the fall of apartheid and the birth of a new democracy, South Africa remains a turbulent and traumatised society.

As Singaram's passage from 'Man of the House' (which I quoted earlier) suggests, a gloss over any of our newspaper headlines will only serve to confirm the extraordinary levels of violence and loss most South Africans are forced to contend with and normalise in their daily lives.

The bleak socio-economic circumstances that many people live under ensure that a large swathe of the South African population remains vulnerable to natural disasters, disease, crime and political instability. It is perhaps this proximity many share with death that causes it to feature so candidly and consistently across our storytelling traditions.

What's important to note when reading many of these stories is that in South Africa, loss, grief and the afterlife have many varied cultural and cosmological iterations. This is evident in stories such as 'The Woman Who Buried Rain'; 'African Death, Western Medicine' and 'Zombie' where the dead keep company with the living, and ancestors intervene in events through the realms of dreams and occasional dramatic turns in the weather. Gogos or grandmothers in both 'Zombie' and 'African Death' reappear from beyond the grave as benevolent forces to assist family members in times of turmoil and crisis.

The manner in which certain characters commune with the dead or shapeshift across metaphysical planes should not be shrugged off as magical realist liberties taken by the authors. Too often, when viewed through the prisms of western religious, philosophical and scientific thought, readings tend to write divination and ritual off as mere fantastical folklore.

Rather, I believe we should acknowledge how these acts of storying the world and meaning-making are intimately connected to the spiritual beliefs, practices and well-being of millions of South Africans. The narratives included in this anthology serve to remind us of the varied stories and processes we humans call upon to make sense of – and heal from – the loss and grief that characterises much of our existence.

Across these pages, readers will be afforded the opportunity of embodying and empathising with ten very different South African perspectives. An anthology like this provides us with a living archive, one that documents and celebrates the myriad of idiosyncratic and often magical ways South Africans have come to see, know and narrate the changing world around them.

I sincerely hope Mr Themba would approve of our curation as much as I hope readers will come to savour the many insights offered by these burgeoning storytellers.

Neil Coppen
26 June 2025

ACKNOWLEDGEMENTS

Special thanks to the Dramatic Artistic and Literary Rights Organisation (DALRO) for the opportunity to collaborate on this initiative. It was a pleasure to work with the operations team led by Lerato Serobe and coordinated by Linda Simelane.

Thank you to the ever patient and supportive Wits University Press team, Louis Gaigher, Tuelo Gabonewe, Veronica Klipp, Alison Paulin and Kirsten Perkins. A special thank you to Louis who worked closely with me throughout the mentorship process and came up with the beautiful title of this anthology.

To the University of KwaZulu-Natal's Centre for Creative Arts team – Ismail Mahomed, Siphindile Hlongwa, Thalente Ndlovu and Owethu Dlamini – thank you for all your efforts in the project management of the DALRO Can Themba Merit Award.

Thank you to my fellow judges on the Award panel that included Tiisetso Mashifane, Niq Mhlongo, Lorraine Sithole, Lynn Joffe, Greg Homann and Shafinaaz Hassim.

Thank you to my friends, Dr Joanne Peers and Dr Dylan McGarry for their insights, advice and care across this process.

Most of all to the top ten writers, each of whom sat with me over many Zoom discussions and phone calls to refine their stories in preparation for this publication. It's been a joy to collaborate with and learn from you all. Congratulations to Dyondzo Kwinika, Princess Unarine Rabada, Sebabatso Madibu, Lerato Mahlangu, Rosieda Shabodien, Dashalia Singaram, Jacqui Aires, Megan Choritz, Lethukukhanya Mzulwini and Kamva Majo.

MR DUIKER SANG THE BLUES

DYONDZO KWINIKA

MORNING HAD COME. I wasn't sure it would. Cold. Still. Heavy. I'd written him something. A poem. He hadn't heard it. I needed him to.

I pulled on my black pants. White shirt. Black tie. Socks didn't match. I didn't care. Had to be there on time. I'd never been late. Not for him.

I reached for my scuffed shoes. The calendar hung on the wardrobe.

22 June.

The date sat on me.

It was Themba's thirty-first.

I was going to fetch him. Same day I used to light candles for him. I'd been there when he was born. Germiston Hospital. Held him. Cried. Not from fear. From how innocent he looked. Nothing had touched him. I told him I'd give him what I never had. Protect him.

From the world. From myself. From everything.

For a while, I believed I had. Now, standing there, I knew I hadn't.

Themba loved birthdays.

I remembered his fifth. Evelyn and I threw him a party. He danced barefoot to Brenda Fassie's *Nomakanjani*, arms wide. Slipped between the shacks. No one saw him. Children loitered near the communal tap, waiting for water that came when it wanted. Not when it was needed. Wire cars swerved through garbage mounds. Sewage cut through dirt paths. Flies everywhere. Scuffles broke out. Pebbles scattered. Voices rose. Then *diketo* carried on, near the shack where we found him. He was under the table, cake on his face. Said he'd be famous one day. He was my boy. Their Brown Antelope.

I wished many things for him.

My hands trembled as I set the pot on the paraffin stove. I leaned closer to Marubini. She was snoring. Same rhythm. Calm and clumsy. Same childlike, twisted face. I chuckled. Forgot, for a second, that I wasn't alone.

She arrived yesterday, after Soekie, my neighbour, who often rushed in. Half-drunk. We'd spent the afternoon at César's, though I wasn't drunk. I was numb all over.

'Ousie, Evelyn called,' she slurred. Pushed her glasses up her nose. They slid back down. 'Your Themba's landing at Oliver Tambo.'

I didn't need to hear anything.

'*Ka nako mang?*'

'Before nine.'

Her doek slipped off. She couldn't remember the airline. I did. Swiss Air Lines. He always took it.

I was on the bed, lost in thoughts of him. Of everything that had brought us here. Then I heard it.

Three knocks.

'Ko-ko-ko, Pa.'

I paced to the door. Chest tight. I wasn't ready, I opened it anyway.

Maru stood there. Bag in hand. Her face was blank, except for tired eyes. She wasn't visiting. She was coming home to me. For good.

I saw the bandage on her wrist.

I remembered the afternoon at the SABC in Auckland Park. She was on set for *When Rain Clouds Gather*. Bessie Head's novel adapted for television. Paulina Sebeso wasn't a part she played. It swallowed her.

'I use them.' She didn't look up. 'I'm not addicted, Pa.'

Her eyes shifted to the door.

'When did they become important?' I asked.

She didn't answer, fingers tapping against the chair.

'When people stopped seeing me as Maru. Only Makhaya's wife from TV,' she said. 'When things broke with Themba … that's not for you to know.'

I said nothing.

It wasn't about Eve. Or Themba. Or her work. It was me. I saw it. Compared her to him. Always had.

The candle sputtered. Shadows stretched across the table. Some of Themba's vinyls lay there. *A Brief History of Marubini* among them. The cover worn thin. Title fading. He was Maru's age then. Younger, even. I remembered that night at Untitled Basement in Braamfontein. He'd finished his set. Picked up the record, looked at it, then handed me a signed copy.

'Why'd you name my sister after this?' he asked.

I didn't answer. He already knew.

'I read up on it,' he said. 'I know what Marubini means. A home no one talks about.'

He smiled, not waiting for a reply.

'This'll remind you of what you tried to leave behind. What's waiting for you.'

I thought he meant something else. Not Maru.

She was auditioning then. Told to smile. Sometimes pushed further. She didn't. Never talked about it.

I stopped seeing her.

'Maru: A Pula', a tune from the album, won the 2015 Standard Bank Young Artist Award for Jazz. Eve, Maru and I drove to Themba's apartment in Kikuyu Waterfall. Third floor, Block D. I bought a red papsak wine. He liked it, even when he could afford better. He poured me Three Ships on the rocks. Said it was for old time's sake. We stood on the balcony watching fireworks over Waterfall City.

He asked if I saw Maru the way I saw him.

I think she heard. Or saw. Either way, she dropped a plate in the kitchen. Glass shattered. She said nothing. Picked up her phone. No shoes. She left.

I told him I'd fix things with her. Said she'd get over it. She was moody. Told myself it was timing. She knew I loved her.

It was the last time I saw her.

'I'm sorry, Papa,' she whispered. 'I was broken. Lost. Hopeless. I want to come home. Rebuild what I can hold on to.'

'It's okay.'

I wasn't sure if I meant it. It was what we needed to hear.

I lifted her bag. Then I saw him. A laaitie. Four or five. Silent. Half behind her. I hadn't known. She'd had a child. Raised him. Without me.

What father didn't know he had a grandson?

I had no one to blame. I raised snakes. It was the truth.

I wondered if she'd told Themba. Called or written to tell him he had a nephew. I didn't know what that would've done to him.

I wanted to ask how she found her way back here. Then I remembered. This was home. The place we grew up. The place I tried to raise them. The place we all learnt how to survive, no matter what.

She hurried in. I put her luggage on the bed. Didn't know where to start. Her eyes searched mine, looking for something. Answers. Solace. I had nothing, only silence.

Sandile darted around the shack, laughing. Oblivious to the moment, smiled up at me. 'Is he my *mkhu*... *mkhulu*?'

Maru nodded.

The two-roomed shack held the three of us. Once, it held four.

I stepped outside after drying the basin. The world was silent. Then dogs barked, goats bleated and pigs grunted far off. Rats scurried and cats meowed as they chased them. Frogs rasped in the muck behind the toilets. The first taxi rattled over the dirt road. I caught Umanji's *Moloi* drifting through the windows.

The place slipped past me. I'd spent too much time thinking only of myself.

My beret was heavier. I folded the poem enough for my chest pocket. My hand trembled, and it slipped out. I picked it up, hoping no one saw. Dug a crumpled joint from my shirt pocket. Lit it. Took one or two puffs. The smoke was bitter, stuck in my lungs. I spat it out. Pot smoke hung in the air. I flicked the stompie onto the ground. Stomped it flat.

The taxi hooted as it faded down the road. For a moment, we were back there. Themba and me riding in the back of that sixteen-seater. June. Winter. When boys became men.

The taxi dropped us at the rank down Oranjehof. We took another, which let us off near Wanderers. I caught a flicker of something in Themba's eyes when he saw the hobos wrapped in plastic and tattered blankets trying to keep warm. He said nothing. Trusted me. His hand stayed in mine.

We pushed through the crowded streets until the Park Station sign came into sight. The ceiling arched above us. People were everywhere. Hawkers shouted. Wares. Beanies, socks, scarves. The *Star*, *Daily Sun*, *Sowetan* and *Laduma*. Chargers and cigarettes. Near the main concourse, pantsulas stomped and danced. Spectators roared. Coins clattered on the floor.

We moved past the turnstiles and shops to the corridor after Debonairs. Dr Cajee's office at the corner, ground floor of the old concourse. A worn sign hung above the door. The buzzer barely worked.

Themba looked up at me, eyes wide.

'Why are we here?'

I didn't answer. Told him this was his passage. Something I'd gone through. Something that meant he belonged.

I couldn't explain. Not to him. Not to anyone.

My father wasn't a man. Ma said he was with Samora, fighting for FRELIMO. She prayed he'd return after the war. I never understood. His absence shaped everything.

Since then, I ran. From my country. From myself. From the man I was supposed to be. I didn't want my boy to feel it. He did. Watched me when I wasn't looking. I turned away before it became something.

Cajee smiled and pulled on his gloves, the latex snapping tight. I lifted Themba onto the table. Told him I was there. He could scream if he needed to. He didn't. Stared at the harsh lights while the surgeon did what he had to do. I sat on a chair, flipping through a worn copy of *Soccer Laduma*.

When it was done, he wrapped Themba in bandages. Gave him a sweet. Said he was a good boy. We headed home. Eve and Maru were by the paraffin stove, stirring a pot of putu. The oily smell of boerewors mixed with paraffin smoke hung in the air. On the table sat a bowl of fresh tomatoes, sliced and ready for the stew.

We sat, laughed and ate.

I helped Themba onto the sponge mattress, tucking the threadbare blankets around him. The pain kept him restless, he didn't complain. When sleep came, I stayed by the bed. Didn't mean to. My hands trembled. Throat tightened. I sat there long after the house quietened. Then I cried. Not for what I lacked, but for the man I was trying to be. For the son I'd helped become a man.

I glanced at my watch. Quarter to five. I'd told César I'd be outside his tuck shop before six. Three sections from mine. We had to be at Arrivals. Terminal A. Eight o'clock. I wasn't sure if Eve was going to drive from Sandton to pick me up. Things hadn't ended well between us. She said she needed stability. Married a high-profile lawyer. Sat on the board of Daggafontein Children's Home. I always thought there was something else to it. I never asked. She was the woman people listened to. Coconut, for sure.

I remembered meeting her, outside my tent, where I cut hair. By the bus stop. She was barely eighteen. Pregnant. Tossed out by her family. Pretty, not obviously. Lucky Dube played on a battery-powered radio. The horrible sound filled the space. She said she needed a new start. Asked for a chiskop. Didn't flinch when I cut close to the scalp. Paid me five bob or a rand. Said I looked tired. I didn't sleep that night. In her, I found something close to home. A country I could belong to. Five years ago, I called her. Begged her to answer. I had to tell her our son was leaving for Zürich. Not for his *Duiker Ducks When Startled* tour. Not for leisure. For something else. Something only he understood. She never picked up.

Later, she said, 'He looked exhausted. Lost. He was unravelling.' She lit a cigarette, drew in hard, then added, 'I tried to stop him. I even asked Josh to reason with him. He closed his eyes and looked through me.'

I told her I didn't feel anything for him. Thought he was selfish. I was too. I didn't know if I pushed him or if he was already halfway gone.

Eve confronted me yesterday about the call we both received from Josh.

'Sir . . . I'll be bringing him home.' His voice broke. I missed the rest. Glass hit the wall, then a scream.

My body moved before my mind caught up. One moment I was on the phone. Next, I was at Soekie's door, falling into her arms. Everything hit at once.

The call took me back to that Christmas. Eve phoned. Said Themba missed a couple of gigs. Told me to search for him. I ran down the streets of Yeoville. Through Hillbrow. Past Bertrams. I found him at Domus Peccati.

High. Eyes dead.

He didn't recognise me. Not at first.

'I'm fine, Papa,' he said.

He wasn't.

He didn't know where the light had gone. It had gone long before.

'I want to fly, Papa,' he said. 'Leave all this behind. Slip through the cracks in the world. Float away. Wherever the sky takes me. Until I'm nothing.'

I heard it for what it was. It wasn't freedom he wanted. It was escape.

Eve stood at the door, arms folded. Dim glasses caught the light, black doek tight around her head, shawl over her shoulders. I was a mess, unkempt, eyes hollow, had not eaten or slept since the call.

She stared at me. Said nothing.

'What's wrong, Eve?'

She shook her head and stepped inside. 'The call from Josh,' she said. 'You knew about it, didn't you, Ebenezer?'

I said nothing.

Her voice dropped. 'So this is how you were going to do it? Bring Themba home without telling me? Without asking?'

She paused. The edge softened. It didn't disappear. 'Ag man, sies.'

'The same boy you never wanted anyway.' I let the words hang. 'Eve –'

Her hand rose. The slap was light. Desperate, not angry. My cheek burnt.

'He was mine,' she said, trembling. 'Not yours.'

It hurt. I didn't move.

Soekie and some neighbours stepped in. Told us to stop. Said it wasn't about us. Said it was about him.

Themba.

I looked at her again. We were older now, tired. I saw the woman I knew. The one I lost.

Without thinking, I reached out. She didn't pull away.

'I wish I'd told you', I said, looking down, 'how much you mean to me. How different my life is because of you. Because of the children.'

She didn't answer. Only stared.

'I'll make arrangements,' she said. '*Ke tla o letsetsa* when everything's ready.'

I didn't know if she would. I hoped she would.

I didn't realise how fast I'd walked from my shack to the shacks at the edge of Section B. Stopped near Soekie's yard. Her gate hung crooked, held up by a bent coat hanger. The rosemary bush at the corner reeked of dog piss. The grass near her stoep was gone. Hard ground now. Scattered with bottle caps, broken glass, burnt-out cigarette butts and bones.

She used to work the Brakpan route before the ulcers took her legs. Now she sold atchar and chakalaka in old jars. Loose draws. Let people charge phones off her car battery. Kept her curtains closed most days.

I leaned on her wire fence, palms pressed flat, breathing through my mouth.

The dogs barked before I saw them.

Four of them chased two tsotsis down the alley behind her place. The thugs clutched bits of scrap. I saw rusted copper rods, part of a basin stand, even brake parts. Stolen. The dogs barked. The boys jumped the ditch and ran for the wetlands.

I knew them. The Jealouz Boyz of Daggafontein. I'd seen them near the scrapyard by the Blesbokspruit. Faces half-covered. Hands never empty. Always watching. Waiting.

Themba was that way now. Something watched me from the edge. A shadow I couldn't reach. I didn't understand how he'd left. He was running. From something. From me. From himself. From here.

It wasn't always like that between us. Things changed. Slowly at first. Then all at once.

He was meant to come home for Easter. He arrived late. Stiff in the wheelchair. Pale. Hands trembling on the armrests. Said he'd been mugged.

I asked why he didn't call me. Or Mme. We could've met him at the stop. He shrugged. Said Wendy dropped him close by.

'Themba,' I asked. 'Who did this?'

'I . . . I don't know, Pa.'

I left my beer half open on the table. Grabbed his arm and wheeled him out. He tried to speak. I didn't let him. Held the lamp. The glow swung across the ground as we moved.

We cut through the settlement. Past the rows of *mikhukhu*. Torn laundry lines. Kids out, playing *mokoko*. Shouting. Dogs barking near the pit latrine. Eve called after us from the stoep. I didn't stop.

The ground was soft ground near the stream, full of muck and the stink of stagnant water. The lamp flickered in the wind. We found them where I knew they'd be. Huddled under the gum trees near the reeds. One was drinking from a papsak, the others passing a *bottelkop* between them. A radio sat on the tyre beside them, blaring Mandoza's *Nkalakatha*. They were laughing. Swaying to the beat. Shoulders bouncing.

They saw me coming. Didn't move.

I moered the first one in the mouth. His teeth snapped against my knuckles. Another tried to grab me. I kicked him in the gut. They scattered. One pulled an Okapi knife. I didn't back off. Swung again.

I wanted them to feel the weight Themba carried.

He stayed behind. Eyes wide. Terrified. Not of the thugs. Of me.

'Papa... please don't,' he said, voice shaking, trying to wheel himself forward. 'Stop, please.'

The tsotsis ran off into the dark.

I picked up his practice journal. Pages torn. Some creased. Ink smeared. He said nothing. Looked at me. Silence filled the space.

For years, I told him what it meant to be a man. We didn't raise hands. Strength was in holding back, not in throwing.

Then I showed him something else. Blood on my knuckle. I wiped it on my trousers. Some of it wasn't mine.

He didn't flinch. Coiled back. Arms folded. Shoulders drawn in. I was something he'd seen before. Something he never wanted to be.

I didn't speak. Walked.

He followed.

We passed Eve again. She didn't speak either. Her shawl tight around her arms. Face blank.

The night waited. It knew what had happened.

It was half past five when I passed the laundry flapping against the fence near the park in Section C. Themba said it was his favourite section. Out of the four. Said it was quiet. He liked the merry-go-round. Rusted. Off-centre. Watched it spin. The April before he left, he'd asked me to drive him there. After what happened with Wendy. Backstage. Cape Town Jazz Festival.

We sat on the cement block near the jungle gym. Watched the birds in the trees. Hadedas, mostly. The sunset didn't last. He opened a Black Label. Took a long sip. Dug into his wallet. Pulled out crisp notes.

'Here,' he said. 'I want to thank you. While we're both here.'

'What for?' I frowned. 'There's no need. *Ha o nkolote letho.*'

I took a long sip. Then reached out. Rubbed his back.

'If you think you do, then let it be to live your truth.'

Then I saw it. Guilt. He knew. I hijacked bakkies. Robbed delivery vans. Looted spaza shops during protests. Stripped copper from broken streetlights. I needed *machankura*. Had to get him his first keyboard. A second-hand Casio.

I remembered taking him to Kippies. Newtown. He must've been ten or eleven. The look on his face when he saw that grand piano in the corner. Something clicked. He belonged there.

Some nights we stayed up till one, two, three in the morning. I'd sit on the bed. He'd play a chord, turn around, ask if it sounded like church or stokvel. Then play it again. Faster. Slower. Laughing. I said nothing. Let him play.

'Don't worry, Papa,' he used to say. 'One day I'll take care of you.' He'd smile then. '*O tla bona.* Get you a house in Selcourt. A gold Casio watch. A Cressida. A trumpet.'

He remembered things I'd forgotten. The way I used to talk about that car when I was drunk. He saw something in me. Something I didn't see.

The house he said he'd buy me never happened.

I pictured it sometimes. Beige curtains. A veranda. Two chairs. Facing the street.

The Cressida. I never drove it.

The trumpet.

Some nights, I thought I heard it. A note or two. Then silence.

I told myself it wasn't finished. There was a song left in him.

We finished the case. Smoked through a full packet of Stuyvesant. He told me things. About contracts. Unpaid royalties. People he'd loved. People he'd hurt. The things he'd seen, the things that followed him. He called them ogres. Shadows with teeth.

Said Wendy caught him and Josh. It spiralled. She smashed his piano. Smashed the windscreen of his Jetta. Screamed. Dragged him by his dreadlocks. Some tore out. He pulled her down. From his wheelchair. Forced her to the ground. Ripped out her braids. Hit her. She didn't get up.

She told the *Daily Sun*: 'Brown Antelope didn't love me. He used me. I did the bookings, the management, everything. He lied. Bonked around. Snorted coke with washed-up kwaito boys in Melville. Sometimes

Hillbrow. Broke me. Slowly. Said the music came from pain. Chaos. It worsened.'

She didn't report it. Afraid of the backlash. He was arrested anyway. Assault with intent to cause grievous bodily harm. He counter-charged. Damage to property. Assault. They dropped them all. Nobody wanted the drama.

He wasn't perfect. Neither was I.

He saw what I did to Eve. The shouting. The bruises. The nights I stayed out. Kids don't forget. Even when they try. The damage stays. Changes shape. Follows them. What did I think would happen?

On the way back from Section C, we talked longer than I thought we would. Old shows. Gigs that didn't work out. Politics. He laughed. A sound I hadn't heard in years.

Then *Diaraby Nene* by Oumou Sangaré started playing. He turned it up. We bounced our heads to the beat. As I tapped the steering wheel, trying to catch the rhythm like *van toeka af*, I remembered him telling me about places he'd been. The sounds he'd picked up along the way.

We drove past a boy splashing himself with a bucket. Two drunk uncles bickered over morabaraba. A haggard woman scrubbing blood off her stoep. Baby tied to her back. Not far off, mealies roasted over a charcoal stove. The smoke filled the air.

When we got home, I stepped out first. Pulled out his wheelchair from the boot, unfolded it. Placed it on the back seat. Close enough for him to reach. Then helped him slide across to the driver's seat.

He sat still for a moment, then looked at me.

'Okay, Papa. I love you. Forgive you. For everything.'

I said nothing. I nodded, gripping the car roof to steady my shaking hands.

He reached through the open window, fingers brushing the door handle, then stopped.

'Let's have breakfast soon. Mugg & Bean. Before I leave.'

I stepped back.

He raised a hand.

'I want you to meet Josh. There's something I need to say.'

He shifted the car, pulled off slowly. Then dust rose behind him, swirling in the fading light.

Five minutes from Césabantu Cash & Carry. I wondered if Maru was done. I'd told her César and I would wait outside the shack before half past six. I didn't want the traffic to hold us up.

I thought about last night. I'd stepped out to light a joint. Smoke rose, curled in the air. I walked to the pit toilet. I needed to pee. Needed a moment away from everything.

By the time I arrived, I became lightheaded. Sank down, back against the door. The stink clung to the air; I barely noticed it. My body shivered. Then came the tears. I curled into the dirt and let them fall.

Rodents scurried over my legs. My chest jumped. I didn't scream. Didn't move. My fear sat there.

I thought about ending it. Not from courage. Something else. Letting go.

The zol had burnt out somewhere behind me. Smoke hung thick. I wanted something to hold on to. There was nothing.

Then I heard footsteps. Reached for my Okapi knife. I'd forgotten it.

The steps were slow. Familiar. Maru.

I tried to stand. Legs buckled.

She didn't speak at first. Placed her hands on my head. '*Ho lokile, Ntate.*'

I was kneeling. Mud on my knees. Tears on my face. Her thumbs moved along my scalp. I was a child again.

She didn't pray aloud. Her hands did.

I remembered her prayers. For Themba. For Eve. Always soft. She knew words couldn't reach them.

A car passed in the dark. The engine dragged. Headlights swept across the shacks. *Ho Lokile* played low.

I thought of Themba. What I never told him. What I never asked.

I didn't ask Maru to forgive me. I didn't ask for anything. I let her hold me.

Later, she said, 'We fetch him tomorrow.'

I nodded. The silence was enough.

Six on the dot. César was already waiting by his Toyota bakkie. Engine running. He ran things around here. The rent he extorted left us bleeding. He'd turned into a comrades. Fat off our backs, rotten, dead eyed. I'd told him about my boy. He said he knew I'd do the same for him.

He held something in his hand. I looked, then looked again.

'*Ndithenge umlahlankosi, mfokabawo,*' he drew on his Stuyvesant, smoke curling around his words. '*Alwehlanga lungehlanga*, Duiker. It'll pass, bra. Hold on.'

He said it the way men did. It was all there was to say.

Eve suggested he get umlahlankosi from the herbalist in town. The buffalo thorn. For the spirit to find its way home. I nodded. Didn't say a word.

I kicked a trash can. Thought about the last time I saw Themba. Blamed myself for how he'd left. For what his country wouldn't let him do. Said we had a right to life, not the right to leave. I kept going over our conversation. Mugg & Bean. The morning was cold. Not the weather kind, the kind that stayed with me. He meant to leave me with it.

I'd expected Josh to be younger. Themba's age. He wasn't. He was older, tall, thin, scruffy. Hippie-ish. Said he lectured drama at Wits. I saw nothing of that in him. He looked at my son like something broken he wanted to shape for himself. Themba didn't pull away.

Josh said nothing. Tapped Themba's shoulder. Reached into his pocket. Pulled out a cloth. When he saw the tears starting to fall, he handed it over.

Themba's fingers closed around the cloth. Then he let it slip back into Josh's hand. He looked at me. Tried to speak. Nothing came out.

We sat by the window. No one said much. I glanced around, trying not to look at him. A painting of a baobab hung on the wall beside us. Branches stretched across a sunset. I stared at it. Hoping for a sign.

Then he said it. 'I'm moving to Switzerland.'

I blinked. 'For what?'

'For … the ending.'

'*O reng?*' I frowned. Shook my head. 'You think you can leave?'

His face was puffy. Eyes dull. Shoulders low. Hands folded on the table, fingers twitching, unsure where to rest.

'I'm on the list,' he said. 'The pain … it'll stop there. It's legal. Takes time.'

I leaned back. Tried to understand.

'You're twenty-six. This isn't real.'

He looked down. Not at me. At the table.

'It's not the wheelchair,' he said, voice low. 'Not even the pain. I … can't anymore. I don't sleep. Breathe. It's like … there's a war inside me. Nobody sees it. Not you. Not Mme. Not Maru. Not even Josh.'

'When did this start?'

'Wits. Second year.' He closed his eyes and, for a second, I thought he'd cry; he didn't. 'I ended up at Charlotte Maxeke. Slit my arm. They said it's something I'll live with. Meds. Therapy. The ups. The crashes. I'd feel alive. Then nothing.'

I wanted to ask him why not hold on, fight, carry the pain, let it win.

'You don't have to,' I begged. 'We … we can fix this. Slaughter –'

I didn't finish. I think he heard it.

'You don't get it,' he said. 'You never did.'

I wanted to say something. Anything. Nothing came out. I reached for my coffee. Cold. My stomach churned. I wiped sweat off my hands with my pants.

'I'm not doing this for attention, Pa,' Themba didn't raise his voice. 'I've tried. *Ha ke sa khona.*'

For a moment, the café carried on. Clinking cups. Murmur of voices. I barely heard. He didn't look at me the way he used to. The love that once held us had slipped and left only silence.

I reached for his hand. Cold. He didn't pull away; it felt distant. I squeezed harder than I meant to. He winced. Didn't let go.

I held on. Like I could stop it. Stop time. Stop death. Stop the leaving.

'If you do this,' I said, wiping my nose, 'then I'm gone, too.'

He smiled faintly, worn down. Bleak eyes.

'I know, Dad.'

It was noon. I didn't realise we were crying until Themba asked Josh to wheel him away.

Josh stood, pulled his sleeve over his hand and wiped Themba's mouth. Then tucked the cloth back in his pocket. Didn't look at me. Took the handles of the wheelchair and turned it.

'If it takes long,' I said slowly, 'if things change … you can always come home.'

Themba nodded. Then said, 'That's the part I'm scared of.'

Outside the Chicken Licken near the Rosebank Gautrain Station, I asked Josh to stop.

Themba looked up.

I knelt in front of him. Knees cracked. People passed. No one looked.

I put my hands on his knees. He leaned forward. Our foreheads touched. My eyes stung. I pulled him in.

His arms were thin. I felt the bones. I held him. Tight.

Josh knelt beside us. Rested his hand on Themba's back. No words. The three of us. In that crowd, in that smell of chicken and petrol.

Then it was over.

I stood. Cleared my throat. Took a step back.

Josh wiped Themba's cheek, then gripped the wheelchair handles. Slowly, he pushed the chair down the narrow ramp beside the stairs into the underground concourse. Wheels scraped the concrete. The chair jerked now and then. Josh leaned in as the slope pulled Themba away from me.

I followed. Not fast. Not slow.

The crowd moved. Bags swung. Phones to faces. Turnstiles clicked. Fluorescent light. The speaker's voice, cutting through.

I kept walking. Eyes searching.

I saw Themba again. He wasn't waiting for me. He saw me. Once.

Josh guided him through the wide gate, then to the lift.

Themba didn't move his face. The door closed.

I stayed where I was. His warmth on my shirt. As if he was there. For a second, I let myself believe he hadn't left. I turned. Moved back through the crowd. Up the stairs. Into the air. I lit a loose draw. Took a puff. He was gone.

The winter sun was out, low and cold. César stopped beside my shack. He hooted. Maru stepped out, wrapped in black, doek on her head, Basotho blanket over her shoulders. Her eyes were tired behind lenses that didn't hide much.

Maru and Sandile climbed into the front with César. She managed a half-smile. It didn't reach her eyes.

I stayed in the back. Hands clenched against my knees. Watching them. I didn't trust him. Not with her.

We drove back to Soekie's. I knocked. She opened. Looked at me, then at Sandile. I asked her to take him. She nodded and stepped aside.

The road was rough. Air full of dust and petrol. My heart stayed tight.

I thought of Themba. His face. His body. His absence. Would I recognise him?

I closed my eyes. Fear stayed.

Behind the bakkie window, I heard Zahara again. *Loliwe.*

I glanced at my Casio. Themba's gift for my fortieth. He'd smiled when he gave it to me. Said life began then.

I wondered if he believed that.

Tick. Tick. Tick.

I pulled my knees up to my chest.

César took the R24 turn-off. The airport sign blinked.

The sky was clear. The moment close. I hadn't said what mattered.

The morgue was cold. Lights too bright. Chemical smell everywhere. Beneath that, something older. Metal clicked. Someone whispered.

A woman in scrubs met us at the door. Said nothing. Routine in her steps.

Handed us forms. Pointed.

Eve and Josh inside. They wore black. So did we. It wasn't their clothes, I noticed.

It was their stillness.

We stepped in.

The casket was polished kiaat. Deep red. Lid half-open.

Themba lay inside. White *umnazaretha* robe. Starched. Hands folded across his chest.

I remembered those hands chasing notes. Shaping sound. Not this.

Eve spoke first.

'Whenever you're ready,' she said. Her voice cracked.

'We'll let him go together.'

She nodded. Waited.

I said nothing. Stepped closer.

Josh stood beside me, his hand resting lightly on my shoulder. He pulled a cloth from his pocket and handed it to Maru.

I reached into my pocket. Herb in my palm, dried and crumbling.

The poem slipped as I tried to unfold it.

Themba would've laughed.

Maru did. Eve too. So did Josh.

Everything slowed. We saw it.

How Themba must've carried it. All eyes on him. No one with him.

Eve's hand rested on my back. Maru and Josh held mine.

We all shared it.

We'd all failed in some way.

Tried to escape the blues. Ended up singing the song he left behind.

The one that stung.

It was mine to lead.

'Little Brown Antelope,' I said, voice low.

'Born of this land.

We are here to carry you home

To the bones that remember.

To the dust that holds your joy,

Where your name echoes off uKhahlamba.'

ZOMBIE
LERATO MAHLANGU

SIX MONTHS AGO, GUSTS of air gathered and twirled into a black tunnel and came charging at me like a two-horned bull at a bullfighting tournament in Spain. Seeing that it was small, I thought the whirlwind would quickly pass by as was normal in the big field where I watched Milani and the Emalahleni under-12 boys play against the boys from Middelburg Primary.

The wind grew stronger, picking up dust, sand and dirt. Taller and taller it rose, moulding itself into the shape of a tunnel before spinning across the open park, halting the soccer game, causing chaos. The crowd of spectators fled. Doris and I grabbed our snacks and hurried away too, but the wind seemed hungry for me, salivating at the corners of its mouth, charging at my feet.

When I was a little boy growing up in Ackerville, uGogo and I used to travel by foot past a similar, dustier open field on our way to church in Lynnville Hall. Whirlwinds were not uncommon in the fields where she and I crossed. It was said that places hit by them belonged to the Mermaid Queen of the water creatures, who was forced to migrate to wetter lands after the government built property on her territory.

Every now and then the Mermaid Queen returned to exact her revenge by sending a whirlwind to punish those who defiled her sacred land. uGogo used to share those tales with me, while teaching me to spit at these whirlwinds when they came charging at our feet.

'Spit, Wanda, so it doesn't sweep you along with it,' she commanded.

In that moment, remembering uGogo's advice, I spat at the whirlwind till my mouth ran dry, but it pursued me still, twirling around my feet, locking my ankles into chains and pulling me into its gigantic belly.

The crowd yelled, begging the dust devil to have mercy as I twirled, hitting objects it had dragged inside its belly. I hit a gate, a car tyre and I may have even collided with a dog. My hearing ceased, but there was a loud ringing in my ears. Through little gaps in the tunnel, I saw the crowd below pulling out their smartphones and snapping pictures of me.

They created hashtags in my name … begged the storm to release me, but it only squeezed me tighter in its invisible arms. Breathing became difficult. My eyes filled with dust and my body felt like a vacuum, shrinking and sucking itself in. I floated higher and higher into the sky.

I was carried across Duvha Park until I disappeared. News of my 'accident' was covered in the Emalahleni paper. Search parties, friends and family looked for me in bodies of water, inside ditches and on rooftops, but I had vanished from the face of the earth. They held vigils for me at night, lit white candles and prayed. Still, no traces of my body were found. My family began to prepare for my funeral, but six months later, I returned, a living testament of the existence of daylight sorcery.

* * *

Ramogolo Paul, Baba's older brother, the leading patriarch on my father's side of the family, places one big, rounded hand on top of my head. He presses his other hand against my forehead and prays for me.

'*Rea leboha*, Modimo, that your lost son has come home!' His voice is a loudspeaker, blasting and reverberating off the walls of the living room where he towers over me on the Persian rug.

'*Rea leboha*, Modimo, that he is well.' Thunder roars and Ramogolo Paul speaks over it by raising his voice.

'Tonight, Patty, Milani and Doris will all sleep soundly knowing that Wanda is alive and that he is well!'

A small congregation of twenty surround me in the living room. They shout 'Hallelujah!' reciting soft, tongue-twisting incantations after Ramogolo Paul.

'The Devil tried, but the Devil failed. And to the Devil we say, Fire!' He presses his palm harder against my forehead, forcefully shoving me onto the rug. I lie flat on my back, staring up at the ceiling.

Ramogolo Paul's skin glows, his suit fits him to perfection and his shoes glimmer like mirrors. The golden jewellery on his body, the double chains around his neck, the stack of bracelets around both wrists and the fat rings lining all his fingers make a hypnotic cling, cling, cling sound.

'Fire!' he shouts at the Devil. 'Fire!' he punches the air.

'Fire!' the congregation echoes him.

And cling, cling, cling, his jewellery sings, a tambourine to their hallelujah. I listen to the sound of the jewellery, to his voice echoing in the living room and wish that this deliverance would end soon.

'Amen!' Ramogolo opens his eyes, lifts me up to my feet, smiles and kisses my forehead.

After the prayer, Ma serves Ramogolo and his congregation tea, scones and jam tarts, a token of her appreciation for the generosity he has shown my family since my disappearance. I stare at Ma's fat scones, the apricot jam hardened on the tarts. I become nauseous. This surprises me as I never had a problem with scones before my disappearance. My tummy groans. There is a battle going on between me and my body.

I rush to the bathroom and vomit air. I splash ice-cold water on my face, staring at my reflection in the mirror. There are dark black bags under my eyes, paleness in my dark brown skin and death in the whites of my eyes. I glance at the shadow standing behind me under the fluorescent lights, a scrawny and weak version of me. The shadow exits the bathroom before me and I quickly follow suit.

Before he leaves, Ramogolo Paul instructs a woman in her early twenties called Caroline, a leader of his church's worship group, to take a picture of all of us. Caroline enthusiastically pulls her Canon camera out of her bag.

'Say hallelujah!' she shouts as she snaps the picture, but the sound of the shutter makes me cringe. My body tingles and my hands tremble. Ramogolo Paul catches a glimpse of my restlessness and squeezes my shoulder to comfort me.

'Say hallelujah!' Caroline, the bubble of joy, cries out again.

The flash on her Canon goes off. I feel a sudden urge to let out a roar or a growl. I want to lunge at her and dig my claws into her caramel skin. I want to crush her camera until it is black dust. I want to stomp on the congregation's heads, on Ma and Doris, unleashing the madness I feel bubbling up inside. But I do not wish any harm on Ramogolo; I've developed an affinity for him. He is, after all, the only one who seems to understand what I'm going through and how to calm me down. After the photoshoot, Ramogolo and his congregation begin to leave.

'You're going to have to get used to a few changes in your life,' he whispers as he makes his way towards the door.

'What does that mean, Ramogolo?' I ask.

'You've been gone for a while, Wanda. It's normal to act out of character,' he says.

'Not many people … I mean, no one ever survives what you went through, never doubt the power of the Almighty,' he says, patting my shoulder. 'I'll come see you in a few weeks.'

Cling, cling, cling, sings his jewellery, a tambourine to his goodbye. Caroline opens the driver's door for him, he climbs in and his Mercedes Benz swerves off into the drizzling rain.

* * *

I lie awake at night trying to connect the thousand scrambled pieces of what has just happened to me. uGogo spat at whirlwinds, saying they were as dangerous as oversharing your dreams with the wrong people. She explained that while those vortexes were often sent by the Mermaid Queen for her own revenge, sometimes people went to the water's edge, appeasing her with sweet treats and silver coins, begging her to unleash hell on their enemies. So, who summoned the dust devil for me? How many coins were used to corrupt the Mermaid Queen?

I lie in bed looking over the pictures Caroline has sent via WhatsApp. I look like a dead version of myself, a corpse. I throw the phone onto the sideboard and begin to count sheep.

'Ramogolo Paul is quite the Evangelist, neh?' Doris asks. I turn, startled.

It's been a year since she and I shared a bed. I often wonder if she's been slowly falling out of love with me. She won't admit it, but I know it's because I don't earn much and, considering that she and I have been together for fifteen years, she's afraid that I'll never be able to afford paying lobola. She often describes our love-making as vanilla, says I lack creativity and rhythm, suggesting that we add sugar and spice to our bedroom activities. She's shared her deepest fantasies with me in the past, the kind that would shame her mother. I often tease her that she's a religious woman, so she has no business bringing kinky ideas into a bedroom she no longer desires to sleep in.

'What?' I ask.

'Ramogolo Paul,' she repeats. 'He's quite the evangelist, neh?'

'I guess,' I mumble.

'And he looks good, too. He's got that thing.' She smiles. 'I don't know, he's more present than your father.'

'What I can't understand is that before the wind swept me away, his church had nine people, including you and Ma. When did he become such a big shot bishop?' I ask, curiously.

'He was ordained after you left,' Doris replies. 'Jealous?'

'No. Why does he have to wear all those chains?'

'It's important that he looks the part.'

'Which is?'

'A man with many blessings. Your uncle is rich, Wanda.'

'I'm sure you wish he was yours,' I mumble.

'Come again?' Doris sits up, daring me to repeat what I just said.

'I just mean, he was Lazarus before I disappeared,' I explain.

'Yes, well now he's Solomon.' She turns her back to me, leaving me alone and disorientated with my thoughts.

* * *

I dream that I'm wide awake in the dead of the night, soaring over rooftops, defying gravity. I'm leaping over suburban fences, rummaging in yards I've never seen. I'm confronted by big, fierce dogs. They bark when I approach and try to bite my legs, but after taking one look at my grotesque face they cower behind trees. I slide through keyholes as if my body was the size of an ant. I do not harm the inhabitants. Around their bodies hover balls of light, green and bright like fireflies. These balls are the metaphysical things that make us whole, blessings that remain undetectable to the human eye, so why is it that I can see them?

I grab these balls of fireflies and stuff them into a kudu skin knapsack and begin leaping over rooftops. I travel across the town and land in Modelpark, in a big house, in a grand estate. I transfer the balls of fireflies into a pair of big, rounded hands, though the figure's face I cannot make out. The owner of the hands blows a small horn into my ear and I'm whisked away into thin air. I float back into the bedroom and wake in a pool of sweat and aching bones.

* * *

When I wake up in the morning, my neighbour Bhut' Omdala waits for me on the other side of the 'stop-nonsense' fence, taunting me.

'Sawubona, you swine!' he shouts.

'Are you talking to me, Bhut' Omdala?' I ask.

'Of course I'm talking to you. There's no one else here.' He points his garden shovel at my face.

'What's your problem?' I snap and turn away from him.

'Yah, walk away, you son of a swine!'

'Bhut' Omdala, watch yourself! I respect you, but now you're trying me!'

'I saw you last night, jumping over the fence. I saw you on the roof and I saw you fly without a broom.'

I'm shocked by his accusations, but the throbbing in my thighs and the pain in my calves tells me, perhaps he knows something I don't.

'Mhm, I knew that something happened to you when that whirlwind hit you.' Bhut' Omdala shakes his head out of pity.

'Bhut' Omdala, what are you accusing me of?'

'You know what you did.'

'And how did you see me? What were you doing out at night?' I try to flip the script, but he has his story straight.

He tells me that he's become a member of the Community Patrol Forum and that he stays up at night waiting to catch criminals who stalk the neighbourhood. He explains that when he heard a loud thud, he thought robbers were trying to break in.

'But then I saw a scrawny thing hunching over the fence,' he continues. 'I tried to shoo it away by knocking on the window, but the thing just stood there with its back to me.'

'So?' I frown.

'When it finally turned to face me, that's when I saw it was you!'

Bhut' Omdala says I scared him at first and that he went to bed immediately, struggling to fall asleep, thinking that I would come back to terrorise him.

'You can go to jail for accusing people of such, Bhut' Omdala.'

'I'm not accusing you. I'm warning you. Try that shit again and I'll kill you, *sithunzela ndin'*, you crazy zombie,' he threatens.

'Are you calling me a zombie?' The neighbours come out to watch in their pyjamas, sipping on mugs of coffee.

'Yes, you're a zombie. You do zombie things in the night, and I kill zombies!'

'Call me that one more time, Bhut' Omdala and I'll clap you . . .' I dare him.

'Do it again and I'll show you your mother,' he warns me before backing away slowly.

* * *

My supervisor throws me a small party at the office, celebrating my return from the dead. She has bought me a large carrot cake, with Oreo cupcakes on the side. I scoff down three cupcakes and two chunky slices of carrot cake. My supervisor giggles and jokes, saying she's glad that I still have an appetite. I chew softly, slightly embarrassed as my colleagues share in the joke, but the cakes barely touch the sides. I've worked at Home Affairs since I was twenty-four, issuing birth and death certificates. I guess you can say I've always dabbled between the living and the dead. The job is repetitive and tiresome; I arrive at 7:30, have coffee at 7:49 and, once seated at my desk, I start counting the hours until knock-off time.

For lunch, I have a spicy bunny chow from the tuck-shop. As I sit and digest back at my desk, the cling, cling, cling of the cutlery from the lunchroom gently lulls me to sleep. I dream of a big man with gigantic hands, adorned with golden chains, sitting on a golden throne, a wooden mask covering his face. I wash his feet in crystal clear water. He bathes in a tub of water as red as sand with green leaves floating above his torso. The man recites ritualistic incantations, summoning luck and money as the water glides over his body, balls of green fireflies dancing all around him, searching for him, finding him.

* * *

At night Doris and I lie in bed, staring at the ceiling, counting our troubles while disregarding each other.

'What's wrong with you?' I ask.

'I lost my job.' She sighs.

'What? But you've been there for close to ten years,' I say, shocked.

'Yeah, well, people just aren't buying furniture anymore.'

'Why didn't you tell me sooner?'

'What would you have done, bought a couch?' she frowns.

'I could have started saving sooner.'

'It still won't be enough to cover Milani's private school, the car, our expenses and ... my lobola.'

Doris sulks and wipes a tear from her eye. I gently run my hand over her back, her legs, thighs and neck, trying to comfort her. Then we have sex. There is a peculiar intensity in my performance. My body does not feel like my own, every thrust comprising a thought. I think about the dream where I bathed the big man in bloody water, the dreams where I fly at night. Then I think about Bhut' Omdala and the thing he called me in the morning. *Isithunzela.* A zombie. Could it be that I've become one?

I float in the air, my arms and legs tingle, my mind wanders and then comes back home. I'm thrusting in space, body spasms, and then I lie in bed heaving.

'Whoa!' Doris yelps, catching her breath.

'You should get swallowed by a whirlwind again,' she jokes. 'You were a beast!'

In the morning the gate rattles and small stones hit my bedroom window. I hear Bhut' Omdala calling me to come out of the house. I rush out of bed, rub my eyes and find Ma peeping out of the living room window.

'This man doesn't know me ...' I wrap my robe around my waist and head outside.

'Get your hands off my gate!' I warn him.

A crowd stands behind him and urges me to step out into the street. They claim that I've become a menace to the neighbourhood, that bad things have befallen them since my return from the dead. 'Don't shit on me, man!' I warn the crowd. 'Your lives have always been bad!' I retort.

Accusations are thrown at me like stones. Breadwinners are losing their jobs. Students are losing their bursaries, forced to come back home to this small town. Bats infest the cleanest of houses, and money no longer seems to come easily. All this, they claim, is my doing.

'And didn't I tell you not to come on my property?' Bhut' Omdala shouts.

'I didn't come into your ugly house!' I shout back. He and I bump chests. He stumbles and quickly regains balance.

'Then explain this!' he leads me to his backyard. I walk behind him, the crowd pushing and shoving me.

Bhut' Omdala points at a gaping hole in his front yard. I gasp, and then I frown.

'Why is this hole in your yard my problem?'

'Because you did this!' Bhut' Omdala digs his phone out of his pyjama pocket and shows me a video he filmed in his front yard in the middle of the night.

'What am I looking at?' I ask.

'Look,' he points.

The video is still, nothing in the image moves. Where there now stands a gaping hole, in the video, is a large pomegranate tree in its place. The leaves on the tree move gently in the direction of the wind. A shadow quickly passes by and the leaves move in its direction, then the image is still again. The shadow passes a second time, and then a figure unexpectedly hops onto the top of the pomegranate tree. Bhut' Omdala shrieks, as if he hasn't seen the video before. I squint and recognise the silhouette of the figure on top of the tree.

Under the glare of streetlights, my face becomes visible. I start to claw at the big juicy pomegranates dangling on the tree. I break a pomegranate in half with my bare hands and shove it into my mouth, devouring every part of it, the skin, the insides and the seeds. Red juices flow out of the corners of my mouth, eyes agog, almost popping out of their sockets. It's a maniacal scene.

'I've seen enough.' I look away.

'There's more.'

Bhut' Omdala fast-forwards the video.

After I've devoured every fruit on the tree, I eat what's left of it, which is the tree itself. I chew on the leaves, on the stem, I chew on the chunky brown bark. When the tree is bare and naked and all leaves devoured, I pull at its stubborn roots and rip it from the ground.

'Yeses,' a man in the mob cries, as I hop from fence to fence with the tree slung over my shoulders, I soar into mid-air, disappearing like a memory.

'Explain yourself,' another voice shouts from the crowd.

'It's not me,' I protest. 'I mean it's me, but it's not really me.'

I slowly back away from Bhut' Omdala and his angry mob.

'Yah, I told you you're a zombie.' Bhut' Omdala follows me. 'And me, I don't have time for zombies.'

'Please, children of Jehovah. Have mercy. He's been captured by demons,' Ma pleads, going down on both knees in front of Bhut' Omdala and the mob.

Bhut' Omdala tries to lift Ma from the ground, but she bites and kicks and refuses to get back on her feet. The mob's attention shifts to Ma for a moment and I know it's my time to run. I spring out of the yard, leaving my sandals on the tar road.

'*Isithunzela siyabaleka.* The zombie is running!' a woman yells and the mob pursues me, chanting:

'*Shis' Isithunzela.* Burn the zombie! *Shis' Isithunzela.* Burn the zombie!'

'It's not him!' Ma and Doris chant back, but how do they explain my face in that video?

I am a zombie; my body and soul no longer belong to me. My body has failed me, allowing itself to be owned by another. I am a zombie, my shadow has acquired a life of its own. It is weak, no longer a reflection of me, or perhaps a true reflection of what I've become? Zombie! Alive and dead at the same time. Zombie! Captured. Zombie is what I've become. How do I tell the angry mob and Bhut' Omdala that I'm merely a victim of witchcraft when they seem to believe that I am the witch?

How do I tell my family to search for my soul when they'll casually pray about it? Ma prays about everything. She trusts prayer to keep the cockroaches quiet at night. Don't they know that you can't pray away the zombie? uGogo knew strong medicine women and men who could rid me of this curse, but uGogo is no longer with us. I stop running and confront the mob. Bhut' Omdala stands in front of me. I raise my fists in front of my face, bouncing from side to side.

'You want to fight me, Bhut' Omdala?' I ask. 'Then fight me,' I say.

He takes off his shoes, raises his fists and jabs at me. I duck and he hits the air. The mob cheers the fight on, rooting for Bhut' Omdala. He throws another punch and misses. I do the Ali shuffle, making him dizzy and agitated. He tries to kick my quick feet. I knock him to the ground and then, with a jab, I knock his front teeth out.

'Woza, Bhut' Omdala.'

I shuffle on the spot and wait for him to get up. Blood drips from his mouth. He squeals, spits and charges at me, trying to push me down. I pick him up like a sack of feathers and toss him on the ground. He lifts his hand up in the air to surrender. I think of kicking him while he's down, but I decide that it's not worth it. So, I head back home. When the mob lifts him up, he picks a brick off the ground, charges at me and slams it into my head.

'Haaibo, Bhut' Omdala, don't kill him!' shout two women who are part of the mob.

He ignores them and slams the brick into my head again.

My head spins. I see the whirlwind charging towards me again. I flee the scene with uGogo. She is dressed in a cloud white dress and takes my hand, guiding me toward a bright white light. I land in a dark room, a space that appears to be an inyanga's shrine.

'Gogo!' I yell. 'Gogo!' But she's vanished.

All I now hear is the familiar cling, cling, cling of chains.

'Come out, Satan!' I shout again. 'You can't hide any-more! Come out!'

The big man with the wooden mask appears out of thin air. I pull off his mask and he stares, astonished to see me in the room.

'Ramogolo?' I gasp.

'How did you find this place?' he asks.

'I remember it,' I say, looking around the room. 'This is where I was kept after the vortex carried me away.'

'You're not supposed to be here. I didn't call for you,' Ramogolo says.

'It's you, Ramogolo,' I say. 'It's you who summoned the whirlwind for me. You and your inyanga turned me into a zombie!'

Ramogolo touches my face gently.

'You're dead. When did you die?'

'Tsek!' I charge at him, but the gold chains on my arms and legs pull me back and burn my skin. He laughs.

'What do you think you're doing, boy? Heh? You may have found me, but I'm still your master, fool.'

I lunge at him again, but the chains pin me to the ground. He laughs harder, I scream, then the laughter dies, and I see the white light again. I cry:

'Gogo!'

* * *

'His family will be burying him this weekend,' I hear a deep voice say and feel a hand rubbing a warm, wet cloth along my ice-cold body.

'What happened to him?' a second, softer voice asks.

'He and a neighbour got into a street fight,' the deep voice explains.

'Damn, and the neighbour killed him?' The soft voice sounds shocked.

'You should see the neighbour,' the deep voice explains. 'He looks strange though, this man.'

'Strange, how?'

'Look at the cuts on his body, then look at his skin. It's like he wants to be alive.'

'Hayi, what nonsense are you talking now? Are you saying this man is not completely dead?'

'Yes, that's exactly what I'm saying,' the deep voice says.

'Let's finish him off, then,' the softer voice adds.

'Is that necessary?' The deep voice is annoyed. 'This man's family needs to find his soul. He was definitely a victim of *ukuthwebula*.'

They shove my body into a cold fridge. I open my eyes and look around me. All I see is darkness. I am tired of darkness. I kick the door until the two men pull me out.

'I told you we should have finished him off.' The softer voice laughs.

'Give me that syringe,' the deep voice commands.

I scream, but my voice is faint. I fight the two men off me, slapping the syringe to the floor. They try to pin me down. I pick them up and throw them to the other side of the room. They lie still on the floor and groan.

The deep voice grabs the syringe and tries to inject me. I pop his wrist. I strip him of his white coat, cover my naked body and rush out of the room.

* * *

I am a zombie, reincarnated, so I must do zombie things. I walk from the Lynnville Mortuary to a veld in Duvha Park where I rest and eat dry leaves. When the sun sets, I walk to Modelpark and into Riverbank Estate where I fight my way past two strong guards who try to stop me from entering. The dogs growl when they see me walk by and I growl back, watching them cower. Ramogolo's Mercedes and a smaller Audi are parked out front; I assume that he and the family are home.

I peep in through the window and see the television light flickering through the curtain. Ramogolo is in the living room, alone, spread out on the La-Z-Boy watching an old Bruce Lee film. He has a glass of brandy in his left hand and a cigar in the other. He wears a maroon silk robe and slippers on his feet. The keyhole is smaller than the ones I've seen and been through, but not impossible for me to slide through.

'Yeses!'

Ramogolo drops his glass of brandy as I tower over him in front of the TV.

'I didn't call for you,' he swallows hard and searches for his horn.

'You didn't have to,' I say, whispering, trying not to wake his wife and children.

'You made me a zombie, Ramogolo Paul?'

'Wanda, what you're talking about?' he tries to play the fool.

'You like money and power, don't you?'

'Who doesn't? You think I enjoyed living from pay check to pay check, seeing my younger brother sitting on a big veranda there in the suburbs, heh?'

'Don't tell me about Baba, he's a coward.'

'I am a man, Wanda. More powerful and greater than your father ever will be.'

'Then why didn't you take him, Ramogolo? Why me?'

I punch the sofa and Ramogolo flinches.

'Here's a lesson: if the universe doesn't give you the things you want, you get them yourself. It's nothing personal.'

'But it is personal. I'm your brother's son!'

Ramogolo pauses for a moment, then he asks, 'So, what must happen now?'

'Where is my soul, Ramogolo? I want it.'

'Wanda, that's not how it works.' He holds back laughter.

'I want my soul back, and I will find it!'

'Don't get all big-headed, boy. Go get me a glass of brandy.'

I step towards him and grab his face with my hands.

'Wanda, don't do this. I'll give you anything. I'll give you my Benz. Which of the kids' cruisers do you want?'

'I can get those things on my own, Ramogolo. You taught me well.'

I apply pressure around his face.

'Please, the kids are going to varsity. Let me send them off, please. Don't do this,' he begs.

'Shh,' I whisper.

I twist and his neck goes pop!

His horn falls onto the floor and I grab it and stuff it into my coat. An owl hoots on Ramogolo's roof. I glare at a portrait of him, his wife and two sons wearing pearly smiles at his bishop ordination. I put the photo face down and slide out the keyhole again.

* * *

'Modimo, set us free from the demons that torment this family,' Ma prays.

'Cover Wanda in your holy spirit because he floats between the living and the dead. Modimo, look at his face and breathe life into him. I also pray for Paul's family. I pray that they find peace. Paul was too young, he served you and was a good man. Curse the demons that took him, if it was not your will.'

'Tell me,' I whisper to Doris. 'Where's Bhut' Omdala?'

'He's in Bronkhorspruit with his mom,' Doris replies. 'The police are looking for him.'

'So, he'll be back?'

'Of course. He left Lydia and the kids behind.'

'Good,' I say. 'I'll be waiting for him when he returns.'

'Haaibo Wanda, you're scaring me,' Doris whispers, her voice trembling.

* * *

'You know, Doris,' I say when we're alone. 'I can help us find a way out of this mess. I can give you the soft life you want.'

'With what money?' Doris scoffs.

'You know we can live like Ramogolo and those people there in Modelpark.'

'You need serious prayers.'

'Listen to me, dammit! I'm saying we don't have to live like this forever,' I growl, squeezing her shoulders.

'Wanda …' she pulls away.

'Look at my eyes, Doris. Look at my face. Walk behind me in the scorching sun and study my shadow. I'm a zombie. I'm dead, but I'm also alive. It is a curse but it can be a blessing, depending on what we do with it. Depending on who holds the horn.'

'Horn?' Doris asks, frightened.

I take Ramogolo's horn out of my knapsack and hand it to Doris.

'Take this, send me out into the streets to take what we deserve. I'm going to be a zombie forever. At least let me be a rich one.'

Doris looks at the horn. She resists at first, then slowly places the horn between her trembling lips. My eyes say: 'Go ahead.' She blows gently and I dissolve into the air. I see a kaleidoscope of green fireflies floating over every house. I see our future. Oh, how mighty and powerful we will become.

THE WATERMELON CARETAKER
ROSIEDA SHABODIEN

OH! MY. GOD! MY mum was right – I really had lost my head.

That was my first thought as I sat at the edge of the ocean, in a sun-dazed stupor, when sharp cries sliced through the beach air and a flurry of people's fingers pointed towards the waves. The voices grew louder – urgent, insistent.

'Eendjie! Hey! Sieda! Jy!'

For one wild second, I thought it was either my head bobbing in the waves or that George had finally made his way to our beach.

I leapt to my feet, squinting against the glaring sun to see what all the commotion was about. But no – what floated in the water was green, not brown. Not my head. Not George either – no fins.

Still, something was happening. Something significant. And it was floating away.

A ripple of dread, not water, coursed through me. At that moment, I realised this day could tilt either way: it might become our best beach memory ... or the kind I'd carry like a bruise.

I did what I knew best: I bawled. Through the blur of my tears, I saw him – my brother – already in motion. 'Tears aren't going to save you, Eendjie,' he shouted, sprinting toward the sea. 'Swim.'

My brother. My Boeta. We were Irish twins, just thirteen months apart – bound by age, sweets, secrets and well-aimed shoves.

He was *my* Boeta. And I only called him that. It's Afrikaans for older brother, yes, but in our world, it carried weight – who walked ahead, who got blamed first, who got first dibs on the train's window seat (me, of course). But it always felt like he was faster too – always the first to run toward trouble, while I stayed behind, crying or calling his name. But today? He was the one diving headlong into the waves to save the day.

How we ended up on this beach, on that day, in that exact moment, had started with a single sentence.

Two days earlier, my dad casually chucked a delightful bombshell into the dullness of our ordinary afternoon when he said this:

'Tomorrow, we're going to the beach.'

Just like that. No fanfare. No build-up – just those six words.

But the effect was immediate. We stopped playing, chewing, perhaps even breathing. Then the room exploded, and my siblings and I scattered in different directions, seized by a collective zeal in pursuit of our swimming paraphernalia and whatever we deemed essential for seaside bliss.

I started crooning, off-key and under my breath, 'We're all going on a summer holiday, mm, du-du dra-ra' – my voice cracking with glee as Cliff Richard's tune rode the wave of anticipation swelling in my chest. That song always felt perfect for moments like this, when the feeling that nestled inside me needed words to carry the bigness of that joy.

However, in my family, a beach trip wasn't merely a matter of arriving, whether for a day at the beach or camping for weeks – it unleashed a set of meticulous and choreographed preparations. Or so we thought. We weren't the casual 'grab-your-towel-bathers-and-picnic-basket' beachgoers. Oh no! Our matriarch, my mother, was the one who ran the show. And she lived by a 'just-in-case' packing creed, a philosophy that has been passed down through cultural osmosis. Even now, wherever I roam on earth, you would likely see a few bags of various sizes trailing behind me, crammed with just-in-case useful and useless stuff, forever fully ready for life's unexpected twists. But let me circle back to our packing ritual for what was supposed to be a one-day beach experience (or, truth be told, a four-hour beach experience). It would take half the day to get there, and naturally, we packed as if embarking on a month-long expedition. We loaded bags upon bags with all sorts of things: bathers, blankets, jerseys, food, and even more food. And the one item that always – always – accompanied us to the beach was a colossal watermelon.

We were heading to Kalk Bay, a quintessential fishing village with cobbled streets and a mix of majestic stone houses, charming fisher-haven cottages, a few architectural eyesores and a cluster of flats for the coloured fishing community – all these abodes perched on the mountain slopes, all positioned to direct the inhabitants' gaze toward the endless blue ocean.

A narrow, winding serpentine road, just a few metres from the water's edge, winds its way along the base of the mountain. Beside it, a railway track mirrors every twist of the road's curves – two parallel conduits carrying tales of happiness and hardship. At the edge of the village, the fishing harbour bustles, alive with the sounds of clanging masts and colourful boats bobbing as fishermen haul in their catch or head out to sea. Seals slip in and out of the waves, scavenging for scraps, while seagulls shriek overhead, poised to snatch a piece of fish. It forms the final flourish in a picture-perfect postcard of a seaside village. Yet beneath that idyllic, charming façade, the tide still drags out a sorrowful tale.

On the train journey to Kalk Bay, listening with a child's ear, my brother and I picked up political breadcrumbs dropped by the adults around us. I heard expressions of nostalgia and mourning – murmurings of a good life once lived there, before people were plucked from their homes and dumped into bleak, unfamiliar towns. As these stories unfolded in the theatre of my child's mind when they spoke about 'apartheid', 'forced removal' and 'segregation', all I imagined were white men; white men sitting around a grand white table, plotting and planning to bring tears to the eyes of people like us. They laughed. I was certain. They must have.

Imagine relocating a community from Kalk Bay's coastal beauty to sandy, dreary townships lined with rows of small, boxy houses. I bet they guffawed when they extended their cruelty even to the nomenclature of these new settlements. They called it 'Ocean View' even though there wasn't a drop of ocean in sight. Others were sent to distant towns inland, where sand covered the nooks and crannies of the houses, and the scent of salty seawater was replaced with nothingness.

I too heard the struggle of adapting, the strangeness of buying fish when they once caught it themselves, the yearning for the sound of the ocean, the ache of missing neighbours, and the urgency to catch up on what had happened to this one and that one. As I sat there, small and brown, with a head full of puzzling questions and a mind too young to grasp the depth of the grown-ups' laments, I tried to picture what they'd lost. But mostly, I just felt it – the waves of sadness rising, flooding our carriage with quiet sorrow.

Despite my young age, I understood something crucial: we had to thank our lucky stars that nature had conspired in our favour and that a narrow sliver of Kalk Bay beach had been designated 'Non-White'. This strange mercy allowed us, coloured people, to hang out there, even though living in Kalk Bay was an entirely different story. An exception was made for a few coloured fisherfolk families; they were permitted to remain in a specific corner of Kalk Bay, where they lived in tiny matchbox flats stacked one on top of the other.

As these stories floated past my ears, I initially imagined that the apartheid men had kind hearts for allowing some coloured people to stay. However, an uncle's dry remark shattered that illusion: 'The only reason they didn't give us all express one-way tickets out of here is because we catch the damn fish.' A pause descended – then a ripple of agreement.

Like a whale leaping from the waves, Aunty Daphne, gums glistening where teeth once ruled, cackled excitedly to anyone who needed to know, 'Ja, that, that small loophole', she reckoned, 'was just white people's laziness to catch and sell their own damn fish!'

At this point, our fellow travellers laughed heartily, mouths wide open, spittle flying in every direction. And just like that, the mist of sadness lifted, creating room for jolliness to slip through irony's side door. That train wasn't just carrying beach towels and umbrellas; it was crammed with stories. Whole lives wrapped in longing, laughter, love and burdens too heavy to leave behind. It carried people who had been told whom to love and whom not to touch. Yet, they fell in love, made love, and made children. Some of us were the offspring of forbidden entanglements – living proof that love outpaces law. But there we were: riding trains, singing songs, slurping melted ice lollies, fighting over windows and laps, and our bloodlines held whispers of the Khoisan, English, Dutch, German, Irish, French, Spanish, Filipino, Javanese, Malay and Portuguese – or whoever didn't board the ship home but stayed and dropped anchor at Africa's tip.

If we had a speaking bubble bobbing above our heads, it wouldn't say 'Non-White', it would say:

'Unclassifiable Truth'
Skin is the sea's surface – shifting with light.
Lineage?
A sacred roll of the genetic dice.

I only knew it was an exciting beach outing. Years later, walking down the same steep cobbled street as an adult, I began to understand what I couldn't then: my fellow train travellers, they weren't just clutching bulky bags, packed food and sun-warmed watermelons – they were clutching onto memories. They weren't merely bringing their children to the beach; it was a pilgrimage to their past, an act of defiance and an insistence on remembering, an act of not forgetting. The apartheid regime designated beaches closer to our coloured hometowns. But still, the gravitational force of memories ensured that our parents nonetheless undertook that long trek to return to Kalk Bay as if to say: you may steal our homes, but not the footprints we left pressed on these cobbled streets, not the memories of the churches where we were baptised and praised God, not the mosques where our foreheads kissed the green carpet and where we begged for forgiveness for minor and major infractions, not the linger of our songs, and indeed not our ability to remember what was once ours.

Although years have swept away some details, a few memories remain anchored in my mind. Beaches for people of colour came without frills – no amenities, no adequate toilet facilities, no changing rooms, as was the case with Kalk Bay's designated patch for us. However, just around the curve from us, where people were paler, the beach offered luxurious amenities – clean toilets, small wooden beach cabanas, and now I wonder if it also had cafés. I couldn't see it, but I imagined it would have.

Those cute, bright wooden cabanas, painted in cheerful yellows, reds, greens and seaside blue, seemed to me like little homes for fairies. However, they stood sentry not for us, but for them.

What loomed over us wasn't whimsical cabanas but a blunt black-on-white painted 'Whites Only' signboard that stood proudly. It drew a solid line in the sand, an invisible border, so to speak. It dictated exactly where whites could submerge their bodies in the sea and where people of colour could submerge theirs. This inanimate sign, its black-on-white paint never fading, dared us to scale the wall it built in the air, mostly keeping us in our place. Now and then, some brave souls would foolishly saunter across that line, feigning blindness to the sign's message, wading into the forbidden waters. If the uniformed policeman assigned to enforce the 'here-for-whites-only' rule ignored the cheeky coloureds, they swam with giddy delight, half-convinced the ocean felt calmer and sweeter on the other side. But if the police were called, they would drag us out of the water, wet and bedraggled, and the cost for dipping your arse in the wrong ocean water could be steep: fifty rands or upwards. Or fifty days (or more) behind bars.

Even with all it endured – ooooh, how we loved Kalkies. That was our special name for Kalk Bay – Kalkies.

White people called it 'Koulk Bay'. And when we imitated them, we'd curl the 'a' just so, wrapping it around our tongues until it sounded more like the 'o' in pot than the 'a' in mat. Then we'd laugh, because that wasn't our language, not really. Our Kalkies was filled with fish guts, women with arms strong from gutting snoek, and sun, sea, sadness, and even stronger memories.

We didn't just go to Kalkies; I'll repeat it – we trekked like pilgrims. Our sheer devotion was evident not only in the way we stockpiled memories, but also in how we prepared and packed for the journey there.

Years later, I was merrily driving behind an old red Beetle, dented and tattooed with colourful flower stickers, and a bumper sticker that declared, 'Focus on the journey, not the destination'. I laughed out loud, 'LOL', as they say now.

'Spot on,' I said to no one, as the past came rolling in like a tide.

That sticker could have been our family's unofficial beach motto. It perfectly captured the essence of our beach-time creed: meticulous preparation for the journey, glorious chaos in cooking and packing, endless delays and the long, meandering trek. But still – somehow – we arrived, faithful as ever, to sink our feet into Kalkies sand.

That motto was not just a saying – it played out in the frantic beach packing of our departure mornings, which meant that our departure for Kalkies, initially scheduled for 6 am, would be delayed to 7 am, then seven blurred into 8 am. Finally, we staggered out of the front door by 9 am.

The delay was due to a whole host of factors. Besides the extensive – some might call it obsessive – packing for the one-day beach adventure, we rummaged for missing swimsuits, a long-ago stored umbrella, and a lot of food had to be prepared.

My goodness, the food!

Disposable income in the family consistently remained low, making take-out food a luxury reserved only for when Dad and Mum received the occasional windfall of Christmas bonuses from their bosses. A day trip to the beach required my mother to ramp up her culinary effort, applying the same philosophy she used for packing 'just in case'. This meant we arrived with biryani – a spice-infused sticky rice dish blended with succulent meat, all cooked in one pot, whose aroma, when ready, seeped from the pot like sacred incense; crispy fried chicken; sweet turmeric-infused yellow rice freckled with raisins; zesty baked beans that were hotter than the sun, laden with chillies and spices; and, of course, how could one go to the beach without home-baked buttered bread? And naturally, a watermelon for dessert.

As we packed, the house transformed into a hive of activity and a symphony of tremulous sounds: packing, cooking, arguing, playing and laughter colliding with occasional shrieks and instructions volleyed: 'Hand me this', 'Put it in this bag', 'Do not forget the towels'. Amidst this glorious chaos, out of the blue, my father, who sat in the corner of our lounge reading his newspaper, rose slowly, his paper folded in one hand, and declared in his trademark dry tone, 'I'm leaving now.' No flourish. No raised brow. My dad, a silent man in a very noisy house, was never one to waste his time; even inflecting his speech with emotion was perhaps too cumbersome for him. Yet we knew, when he spoke, we abided by his wishes. Miraculously, a hush would fall over the house and bags were assigned; we were ready to leave. As always, I tried my best not to take the heaviest bag and grabbed the towel bag. 'Big mistake,' I thought as I hoisted the bulky monster and staggered beneath its weight, shifting it from one shoulder to the other and learning an everlasting life lesson – choose wisely, or you will carry your burden all the way to your destination.

When we finally stepped off the train at Kalkies, my brother and I were unravelling at the seams. The exciting, albeit exhausting, three-hour journey – part walking, part bus ride, and part train ride – had frayed our sibling bond to a thin thread. We were best friends, unless his friends were around – then he snubbed me as though I were a stranger bothering him. I went right ahead and ignored his disregard for me and wormed my way into his life, whether invited or not. On that day, though, I didn't need to sneak in; I had him all to myself. We were travel buddies. What had started with us walking in rhythm, arms swinging, and playing guessing games on the train had now soured into killer glares. 'Stop it!' 'Move on!' were the refrains since we had grown weary of each other and engaged in shoving matches and elbow jabs every few moments, nearly escalating into a brawl if not for the watchful eyes of the adults. And I'll admit, a lot of it had to do with me. Despite his elder status, in the game of knowledge, the answers sailed out of my mouth, and I was way ahead on the scoreboard.

'How many stations until Kalkies?' he asked. I answered before he could even blink. 'I spy with my little eye' – his eyes could never quite land on what I was spying. If anyone dared to mess with me, he would be the first to step forward, fists raised. And should they come after him, I was there, my voice primed to pitch at such high decibels it would send them into retreat. Back then, he was just my Boeta and my protector; I didn't yet know I'd fiercely want to bottle these memories, to catch them like seawater and keep them in a jar. But here now, on this slow ride to Kalkies, I only had to manage to rein in my competitive streak and pretend I didn't know what he was spying, even though I did

– because he was so silly, squinting at the thing he'd picked as his spy item.

But as we sank our bare feet into the warm sand, the crankiness vanished, and my heart zinged with joy. Just like that, all was well. The din of the beach competed with the boisterous banter between my brother and me. We couldn't contain ourselves ... our favourite hang-out spot wasn't fully occupied yet! The so-called tunnels were actually the archways beneath the railway bridge, and these coveted concrete shade havens offered much-needed respite from the scorching sun and provided the holy grail: shade. From experience, I can tell you that missing an opportunity to secure a spot under the arch-way meant the difference between a first-degree sun-burn, the kind that turns your skin two shades darker and leaves it peeling like cheap water paint flaking off a damp wall, or a second-degree roast that left you burnt as dark as night, blistering into next week and earning you a reckoning for your stupidity; arrive earlier at the beach and wrestle harder for a spot in the tunnel.

But whether we had our tunnel spot or not, the first ritual at the beach unfolded as seamlessly as the waves washed over the shore. Before we could utter, 'Kalkies', Mum would retrieve a large jar of Vaseline from one of the many overstuffed bags. She believed she knew a thing or two about the dangers of the African sun. In her valiant effort to protect us, she dipped her fingers and approached us like a warrior on a mission, proceeding to slather us from forehead to toe with that glossy goop. Vaseline, as you surely know, is an oily concoction that serves less as sunscreen and more as a magnet for beach sand and sun. A mere nanosecond after the Vaseline shimmered on our skin, it eagerly invited the sun and every grain of sand to come in, and they accepted the invitation, transforming us into human koeksisters – glossy and gritty. Mind you, for the longest time, I thought all of this made sense, believing it was what beach life was all about: Vaseline, swimming, sand and sunburn. Oh, how I loved the beach! Or perhaps it was 'Oh, ouch, how I loved the beach'?

Just as the Vaseline started to bake into our skin, it was time for ritual number two: chilling the watermelon.

'What?' you may ask. 'Cool down a watermelon?'

You heard right. The very watermelon, bought from the fruit hawker back home, lugged on the bus, jostled through the train aisles, and carried on a long walk; hoisted on my father's shoulder, then passed to my brother, and back to my father again. By the time it arrived at Kalkies, it was hot and bothered. Since cooler bags had either not been invented yet or were just too expensive for us, the watermelon had no choice but to endure the full brunt of the sun like the rest of us. If you have ever tasted a hot watermelon, you will agree it was never meant to be served hot ... not even for coloured people! This is where the brilliance of black people's ingenuity shone through, as they MacGyvered a way to make the watermelon icy cold, as if it had come straight from the fridge.

An essential part of this ritual was appointing someone to chill the watermelon. On that day, it was my honour to be chosen as 'the watermelon caretaker'.

To chill the watermelon, the caretaker had to follow a few rules. Four, to be precise.

> Step 1: Dig a hole at the edge of the ocean, where the waves kiss the shore, and bury the aforementioned hot and bothered watermelon in the hole.
>
> Step 2: Avoid digging the hole too deep, as the gentle curve of the green top of the watermelon must still be visible.
>
> Step 3: Keep a vigilant watch, as though your life depends on it, while the seawater caresses the watermelon. The sea can trick you and snatch it away. A strong backwash is sly like that and could unearth the watermelon, dragging it into the deep blue ocean.
>
> Step 4: Wait. Perhaps forty-five minutes or longer. Then extract it, rinse it off, and you shall know the taste of an ocean breeze and triumph.

Now, that seems simple enough, doesn't it?

Except if the watermelon watcher is the sort of child my mother would often refer to as a 'loskop' – that was me, a daydreaming, gawky kid. To emphasise my forgetful nature, my mother would frequently warn, 'Eendjie' (my childhood nickname was 'Duckling') 'if your head weren't screwed onto your neck, you would have a great chance of leaving it behind.' This statement puzzled me no end; after all, how does one walk around without a head?

I was that kind of kid, sitting for hours, oblivious to the world around me. This created a dangerous situation: a daydreaming girl 'watching' a potentially floating watermelon. I dug a hole, placed the watermelon in it, and positioned myself as the diligent guardian of the watermelon. Then my mind began to wander off to a more exciting world of seahorses, friends, and one day living in that beautiful white-and-blue double-storey house my eyes had just settled upon. Or perhaps the white cottage next to it ...

It was then that I was rudely snapped out of my reverie by screams.

'Eendjie! Hey! Sieda! Jy!'

Half of the beach, or so my memory recalls, jumped up and moved into action to catch the drowning watermelon as it bobbed further into the ocean, 'Grab it!' 'Swim for it!' 'Hold it!' The commotion was overwhelming, and the scene before me felt as if I was watching a slow-motion movie. One uncle, cursing and half drunk, judging by his zigzagging, uncoordinated swimming strokes, snatched it and held on to it, offering us a toothless smile, and . . . promptly lost it again. The watermelon had broken free once more and headed out as if it had somewhere important to get to.

Then my brother made a dash for it. He ducked and weaved, and after a few failed attempts, he emerged carrying the 'prize' aloft like a golden trophy. He was my hero of the day, my Boeta, my gladiator. He deserved a certificate, 'The Boy Who Saved the Watermelon'. But all he received was thumps on his back. He sauntered past me and said solemnly, 'Eendjie, stop daydreaming. George could've eaten our watermelon.'

For the longest time, my siblings and I thought that 'Jaws', the iconic Spielberg blockbuster about a flesh-loving great white shark, was called 'George'. Who knows how this misnaming came about? All I can recall is my mother instructing us one Saturday morning to get ready, as she was taking us to the cinema to see 'Jaws'. It was probably a combination of our limited comprehension of the English language, compounded by the delirious excitement of hearing the word 'bioscope' – which, in those days, was a rare treat and thus a very special outing – that led my brother and me to burst out of our home and boastfully announce to our friends that we were on our way, 'to watch the movie George'.

After watching the movie, it instilled a fear in us, and we eyed the ocean water with suspicion. We warned each other to keep a sharp eye out for George. My brother, to ensure we remained alert and possibly out of great hilarity at my expense, would often imitate the famous foreboding movie soundtrack whenever George approached his next hapless victim. In a flash, hearing that dreadful tune – 'Duh-duh … duh, duh' – flowing from my brother's mouth transported me to a world where George circled beneath me, eyeing my skinny legs as if they were Vienna sausages. If a journalist had caught me at that precise moment, arms flailing, hot-footing it out of the shallows to escape the imagined George that was aiming straight for my legs, I am convinced the headline would've read: 'Girl Who Ran *on* Water'.

Later that afternoon, all the hysteria and fear were set aside as I had a revelation. I reckoned that since George was a great *white* shark, he would only be interested in eating white people. I shared my epiphany with my brother and our friends, and from that moment on, we splashed and swam as if we were invincible, celebrating our dark skin at the beach. We felt we had one up on the whites, finally. That confidence only lasted until my brother, ever the one who knew precisely how to push my fear buttons, would start humming that ominous 'duh-duh, duh-duh …' – George's siren song. And like clockwork, forgetting my own racially selective shark theory, I would tear out of the ocean.

But for now, I had other things to worry about – not sharks, not even the hungry white variety circling the cold Cape waters, but the looming figure of my furious mum. She wasn't swimming; she was marching towards me. Losing the watermelon, despite her explicit warning to be a vigilant caretaker, had consequences. At best, a tongue-lashing so sharp it could slice through a watermelon; at worst, a swift and unforgettable beating that left red marks not just on my skin but also in my memory.

She opted for both – a smack on the back of my head that echoed down to my buttocks, accompanied by what I assumed was a universally recognised child-discipline ritual. It was a choreography of slaps and rhetorical questions – performed with rising passion and pitch. The dance always began with a deceptively calm voice, punctuated by a precise rhythm as her palm met my skin, and then built into a soprano crescendo worthy of an opera performance.

Mine went like this:

'Did. I. Not. Say –' Thwack! Thwack!

'Watch. The –' Thwack!

'Watermelon?' Thwack!

'It could have drowned!' Thwack! – this one landed squarely on the back of my head.

Then came the grand finale, a breathless cascade of accusations, panic and culinary grief.

'And – what – do – you – think – we – would – then – have – for – dessert!' Thwack! Thwack!

Amid the bewildering thwacking and not yet grasping the rhetorical nature of these questions, I was briefly tempted to answer, 'Ice cream'. However, something – perhaps survival instinct or the disorienting slap to my temple – warned me to keep that answer buried. My brother, an amused spectator, widened his eyes and shook his head vigorously, barely able to contain his laughter. He pressed his index finger to his lips. I understood the silent code: these questions were not an invitation for dialogue; one was expected to endure the thrashing bravely, without flailing, dodging or diving, and it would soon be over. But I was not brave; I dodged, dived and wept rivers.

For years to come, I endured it, so to speak. Tears became my faithful shield. Rivers of tears flowed in response to any harm directed at me. They leaked from me, yes – but they also washed away what was too much for me to bear and could not yet be contained.

In stark contrast, my Boeta resolutely adhered to his decision: he would *never* cry. One day, out of the blue, he declared to no one in particular, 'Tears are for sissies'. I admired him then. My Boeta was so powerful that he could even stop tears from flowing from his eyes.

He chose the armour of silence: stoicism. However, it served as an imperfect shield. Somewhere between boyhood and becoming a man, at the tender age of fourteen – or perhaps even earlier – he discovered drugs that helped him uphold his no-tears promise. It provided him with a false refuge, a way to keep the brutality of the world at bay. It numbed the anguish in his soul and steered him down the path of self-destruction and, bit by bit, I watched him drift away, like pieces of driftwood carried out to sea.

But the Duckling was too young to know how to throw her brother a lifebuoy and simply cried, 'Swim! Swim!' By the time he was cocooned in his white death shroud, his face soft again, finally at peace, I stood over him with tears streaming from every pore and thought, 'Perhaps tears could have saved you.' But perhaps not.

I, a faithful vessel for tears, still weep for him. Sometimes, out of love. Sometimes, to share the unbearable weight of remembering by narrating stories like this – stories that bring him back in fragments: funny, fierce, and beloved.

Grief has its place, but memory – especially the sunlit, sticky kind – holds its own insistence.

So, I return to that beach day, to the moment just after the watermelon's near-drowning and my storm of tears had passed. Calm settled. We gathered to eat the cold, beachy, salty-sweet watermelon. As I sank my teeth into that piece of heaven, it felt like the sweetest and coldest thing I had ever tasted – an elixir for forgetting the beating and embarrassment of being whacked in front of my friends.

Basking in the embrace of the Kalkies sun, the watermelon-red juice lazily traced rivulets down my chest, mingling with the residue of Vaseline and sand on my sun-kissed skin. I hummed, 'We are all going on a summer holiday', pausing every few seconds to expertly spit the watermelon seeds in the direction of my brother's legs, watching them land like tiny comets.

MURMUR BECOMES A WAVE
MEGAN CHORITZ

THERE IS SOMETHING BROKEN about this day. Still air and pre-dawn heat have made me headachy and nauseous. In the courtyard, I discover grey, horny caterpillars on the Ficus, eating their way, systematically, through the leaves, with just the centre stalks remaining. I want to pick them off before every leaf is gone but the thought of touching them makes me squeamish.

My sleeping T-shirt smells of metal and sweat but, instead of taking it off, I put my nose inside the neck and sniff. Riley comes up behind me as I sit on the back step and nudges me with her soft nose. Come. Don't just sit there. Get up. Biscuit. Walk. She knows what will happen if I wait too long.

'Okay, okay. I'm coming.' I stretch and yawn, still waiting for the day to find me. I pull the T-shirt over my head and walk to the bathroom for yesterday's clothes, good enough to walk the dog in. Living alone will lower the bar.

On the street corner at the top of the road there is a small commotion. A crowd. Children in their orange and maroon school uniforms, their mothers, two rough sleepers, a taxi driver and a few of his passengers who have climbed out of the minibus stand around, looking and pointing. Riley and I get closer, and the murmur becomes words.

'Grabbed her handbag.'

'And ran down Barton Street.' It's Washeela, from number 11. She walks her twins to school every morning, even though they are 12 years old now. They always keep a few steps in front of her, distancing themselves from the embarrassment.

'What happened?' My voice is thick from not speaking to anyone yet this morning, except for the dog. Living alone will do that.

'I almost hit him. Had to slam on the brakes.'

'This neighbourhood is getting rough, jong.'

'In broad daylight, nogal.'

Riley and I join the crowd. Some of the nervous kids move away from the dog, even though she is old and passive.

'What happened?' I ask again, even though I know the story will be about a local crime.

'Woman was mugged on the footbridge. He got close to her and took out a knife.'

'Stole her bag and cellphone.'

'Threw her bag over the wall here.' Washeela points over the low wall of a crumbling semi-detached house that has been unoccupied for years.

'I been warning you ous. The bergies been squatting here. Starting fires. Smoking tik and Mandrax.' Tyrone, now clean after years of smoking himself, is the loud voice of disapproval.

'We didn't see him.'

A woman who looks familiar, but I don't know her name, clutches her house keys and a plastic shopping bag.

'I saw him, when he ran across the street. Little guy. Running with the knife in his hand.'

'Did somebody call the cops?'

The taxi driver shifts his weight from foot to foot, maybe thinking that he had better leave before they come and start asking questions. Riley tugs on her lead. She needs to get to the park to make her ablutions and she has waited long enough.

'I sent a message to the neighbourhood watch.' Mabel, the wife of Anwar from the shop, grabs her child's hand.

'The neighbourhood watch.' I sigh. Robbie. My ex.

I leave, letting Riley pull me towards the park. Voices become a murmur again. I stand on something squishy, and look down, expecting dog poo. A bit of rice and meat has spilled out of a discarded polystyrene take-away box. My nausea comes back. I wipe the edge of my sneaker on the kerb.

The day's temperature is already creeping up, even though it is still before 7 am. The green painted metal bench is warm to the touch, and I can feel sweat running down the backs of my legs as I sit, still undecided about whether to do a fast walk around the perimeter or maybe just wait for Riley to do her business, then pick it up and go.

The gate squeaks open. A man in a hoodie approaches the gym equipment and jumps onto the leg and arm machine. His movements are strange and jerky. I think he is high. Riley has stopped sniffing and is staring at him. It creeps up on me, the knowledge that we are alone in the park.

Riley is hunched over in the long grass, typical, to irritate me further, when the man on the machine starts a loud conversation. I look at him and he is staring at me, but I don't know if he is seeing me. He is shouting, arguing with his invisible interlocutor. He has started to sweat, and droplets fly from his face as he shouts. Dark wet patches appear on his hoodie, under his arms and in a triangle on his chest.

'That's him! The guy. He's the guy.'

Robbie is at the gate. Neighbourhood watch WhatsApp group admin. Self-appointed crime watchdog. And my ex. I know exactly how he will behave. Robbie will insert himself, pretend to sort it out. He straddles the border of rough, but just barely legal vigilantism. He is opportunistic in every situation that can show him off as the hero of the 'hood. I cannot bear him. He is pointing at the guy on the gym machine. I have no idea how he knows that this is the guy.

'Hey! You. Get off that thing and come here.' His tone is racist. He will deny it if I say so, but I can hear it. There is a 'this is our park' note in his voice.

I stand to go and pick up Riley's poo and realise that Robbie had not seen me. Now he shouts to me.

'Lynette, get away from that man. He's got a knife. He's dangerous.'

'Fuck off, Robbie. You can't tell me what to do anymore.'

Riley looks from me to Robbie.

'Lynette. You. Are. In. Danger. What. Is. Wrong. With. You?' It is not a question.

Hoodie man has taken no notice of Robbie, or me, and is picking up speed on the machine, his arms and legs pumping wildly.

'Robbie. You don't know anything about this guy.' I can hear my own tone. Trying to de-escalate, trying to reduce potential harm. It's like I am a negotiator, a peace monitor. I am not in the mood for this, but don't know how to stay out of it.

'Get out of the park, Lynette. Let me deal with this.'

A few of the mothers and their kids rush down the road and stand at the gate with Robbie. A cop van pulls up and mounts the pavement. Gym machine guy has not seen them or heard them. He is still shouting, arguing with his invisible adversary.

I bend over and pick up Riley's poo with my plastic bag-covered hand and some of the children titter and giggle. White woman picking up dog poo is always funny.

When I look up, gym machine guy's hoodie falls back off his head. His air pods are visible. Everything falls into place. He is shouting along to rap, hip hop, some shouty jerky music. He has not seen me, or Riley, or heard the growing commotion at the gate. He is training hard. He is not high. I have misunderstood.

But now, the policemen have come through the gate, Robbie at their heels like a terrier. I pick up words, snippets. 'Mugged a woman on the footbridge', 'definitely has a knife', 'threw her bag over the wall'. Robbie has read all of this on the WhatsApp group. He acts like he was there, saw it all.

'Back off!' I shout at the policemen who are unholstering their weapons. It is the wrong thing to do. They cock their guns and yell. 'Hands up. On the ground. Now!'

'Wait! He can't hear you. He's got things in his ears.' I can't remember what they are called.

Riley is confused and agitated. She moves towards me and one of the policemen aims their gun at her.

'Stop!'

Robbie is still behind them, still muttering to them, egging them on.

A crowd has gathered at the gate. 'It's not him!' shouts Washeela.

Someone else, late to the party, 'Who? What's he done?'

'I know that guy! He's a personal trainer at Crossfit.'

'The mugger is long gone, man. I saw him run towards the station.' Tyrone, I think.

'Seen this guy in the park before.'

'Ja, he's tall hey. Must be a foreigner.'

That word is the trigger. I know what is coming. I run towards the man. Riley trips me up and I go flying, face first into the grass. I look up. The man stops, seeing me for the first time, reorienting to where he is, his surroundings. He jumps off the machine. He is agile, graceful, bounding to help me. I see the look of confusion and disbelief on his face as I hear the shots fired. His arms go up as his knees hit the ground next to me and his torso crashes down.

A man on a gym machine has been shot in my local park, on a hot Wednesday morning before 7:30 am. I am lying on the grass in the park next to the body of a man who was coming to help me.

THE WOMAN WHO BURIED RAIN
PRINCESS UNARINE RABADA

The Season of Becoming

Long before the rain stopped, long before the silence crept into the soil, there was music. Not from instruments, but from hearts meeting for the first time. Munei first saw Vhutshilo at the Dzimauli River, where girls washed laundry and boys fished with reed spears. He was barefoot, sun-darkened and laughing with a friend over a slippery fish that had escaped his grip. She noticed his hands first – strong, shaped by earth and effort. Then she noticed the quiet behind his laugh, like a man who had known pain but chose joy anyway.

Vhutshilo noticed her silence. While other girls giggled and tossed water, Munei sat with her skirt hitched up, scrubbing a cloth with slow, purposeful strokes. She didn't smile easily, but when she did, it lingered. Like honey on the tongue.

It took him three visits to speak to her. He asked if she could help him patch a tear in his shirt. She said yes, but only if he brought the needle. The next day, he brought a whole sewing kit and stayed the afternoon, telling her about the shapes he saw in clouds, how he wanted to carve them into wood one day. She said nothing then, but when he left, she traced her finger along the lines he'd drawn in the dust. But the next morning, a carved wooden pendant was left on the stone she always rested on. He had made it. A sun wrapped in rain.

'Why sun and rain?' she asked him a week later.

'Because you will bring both into my life.'

Love came slowly, like water heating over low fire. It wasn't loud. There were no declarations. Just shared silences, looks that held longer than necessary, the way he always left a piece of fruit by her doorway and she began adding extra sugar to his tea.

They were married under the marula tree which Vhutshilo had planted. No ring, just a string of grass tied around her finger. 'This way', he said, 'you'll always be rooted.'

Before the Drought

After their quiet wedding beneath the marula tree, Vhutshilo and Munei built a life filled with small but precious moments. They built a hut with their hands, made from clay and sweat. It was a home where love softened every hardship. They cooked over fire. Laughed into the night. On Saturdays, Vhutshilo carved spoons while Munei sang to the clay pots.

When Tenda was born, they both wept – not out of fear or pain, but wonder. Their life was not rich, but it was full. Full of sound. Full of touch. Full of rain. Tenda brought joy so deep it felt like the earth itself was breathing with them. A boy so curious he once tried to speak to a lizard. He followed butterflies like they carried secrets. He would help his father plant maize, would sleep in Munei's lap with soil still under his nails.

Vhutshilo worked with his hands. He wasn't just a man; he was the warmth that breathed life into the village. He was a craftsman, known for carving beautiful wooden spoons and intricate bowls, his hands skilled not only in shaping wood but also in tending to the fields. He was a provider – steadfast and gentle, with a laugh that resonated like a deep drumbeat. He always had time for stories, whether it was talking to the old men under the shade of the tree or to Munei in the quiet of the evening. He would often say, 'There's no time like now. The work can wait.'

Munei cared for their home and garden, planting seeds with hope in her heart. Their days were full of shared laughter, whispered dreams and the steady rhythm of ordinary life. Their love remained quiet, not loud or showy. It lived in shared silences, in the way Vhutshilo rubbed her ankles after long days, or how she added extra ginger to his tea without him asking. They had no riches but were rich in moments.

But the call of the mines came like a restless wind, promising a better future beyond the horizon. Men left in busloads with hope in their eyes and plastic bags as luggage. Vhutshilo kissed her forehead and promised, 'Just one year, then we'll buy a proper zinc roof and build a home strong enough to weather any storm.'

Yet, as the months passed, the rains grew sparse, the earth cracked and hope began to wither like the drying maize in their fields. The drought was coming, and with it, a silence that no song could break.

He never returned.

A letter came with a red stamp and a name that wasn't his scribbled on the back. An accident. A collapse. No remains sent home. No body to bury. Just silence. Munei screamed that day. So loud the chickens scattered for miles. She beat the marula tree with her fists until the bark peeled. That night, she took the shawl from their wedding night, wrapped it around her shoulders and sat by the fire with her son. She didn't eat. She didn't sleep.

Weeks later, the fever came for Tenda. It stole him slowly. First his smile. Then his strength. Then his voice.

Munei begged the ancestors. She burned herbs. Called for the sangoma. But the fever didn't care. The day he died, the sky was cloudless.

She wept for seven days. On the eighth, she remembered the old sangoma who had once said, 'Grief is not the end of water. Sometimes it is the beginning.' She took a spoon made of reed, collected the tears from her face, and poured them into an empty gourd. It felt foolish. But something told her to keep going. By the time the village declared a drought, her gourd was already a quarter full.

The Village of Dzimauli

Dzimauli had once been called the singing valley. Winds used to rustle the trees like whispers of old songs, and the streams would hum lullabies to frogs and dragonflies. But in the years since the rain disappeared, the only music left was the creaking of thirsty earth and the brittle snap of dry leaves beneath tired feet. Life in the village had become a daily negotiation between hope and survival.

Women woke before dawn to walk farther than ever for water, returning with clay pots balanced on aching heads. Men sat on overturned buckets playing checkers with bottle caps, speaking little, their dreams shelved like unused fishing nets. Children grew up without knowing the sound of rainfall on rooftops or the scent of wet soil.

And through it all, Munei remained.

They called her 'the widow who buried rain'. Children were warned not to play too close to her yard. Some villagers claimed they saw smoke from her chimney on nights with no firewood. Others swore she spoke to shadows. Still, every time a funeral was held, it was Munei who laid down the first stone. She was always the first to arrive, her face expressionless, her hands carrying herbs no one could name. They feared her – but deep down, they respected her.

It was whispered that when a baby was sick and modern medicine failed, mothers would leave small gifts outside her gate – a ribbon, a handful of salt, a song hummed at midnight – and somehow, by morning, the fever would break. But no one spoke to her. Not openly. Munei, for her part, asked for nothing.

She tended her garden though nothing grew. She swept her yard though the dust always returned. She patched the same part of her roof each season, though the wind seemed determined to undo her effort. And every night, she sat beside the hearth, the gourd of tears hidden beneath the floor. Sometimes, in the dark, she whispered her son's name. Sometimes she just listened – to the wind, to the stars, to the quiet groan of a world still turning. She had stopped waiting for rain.

She had stopped waiting for anything. Until the boy arrived.

Tshilidzi's Journey

His name was Tshilidzi, meaning 'Mercy'. A name whispered over him by a mother who'd wrapped him in a blue cloth and set him down on the river's edge early one morning. No one knew where he came from – not even him.

The women who found him swore he was glowing. Not in the way of myth or fireflies, but in the tired way of someone who had survived something too big for their small body. He couldn't have been older than eight when he wandered into Dzimauli barefoot, clothes torn and eyes far older than his age.

At first, no one knew what to do with him.

He spoke little but listened much. His voice was soft, like wind slipping under doors. The headman took him in for a while, but the boy kept sneaking away – drawn by something no one else could hear. They would find him sitting under trees, staring at clouds, humming songs he didn't remember learning. The children didn't play with him. He was too strange. Too silent. Some said he had the eyes of an ancestor.

When he showed up at Munei's gate, she didn't speak. She simply opened the door. He entered as if he had always belonged there. For days they didn't exchange a single word. Tshilidzi swept the yard, fetched water and collected firewood without being asked. He watched Munei carefully, mirroring her movements, her silences, even her way of watching the sky like it owed her something. At night, he would lie on the mat near the fire, listening to the small cracks and pops, while Munei sat with the shawl around her, whispering to shadows. One evening, he finally spoke.

'Why do you talk to the fire?'

She looked at him for a long time before answering, 'Because it listens.'

He nodded, as if that made perfect sense. After that, he began to talk more. Bits and pieces. Fragments of dreams and memories. He remembered a woman with soft hands and songs in her breath. He remembered a scream and then water. He remembered nothing after that.

Munei never pressed him. She simply let him exist. He began to thrive. His cheeks rounded. His feet stopped blistering. He carved small animals from left-over wood. He drew symbols on the ground, symbols Munei hadn't seen since she was a girl sitting at her grandmother's feet. Sometimes, when she wasn't looking, he would hum a melody that reminded her of Vhutshilo. She didn't know if Tshilidzi had been sent or if he had just come – but slowly, he began to stitch warmth back into the cold corners of her soul.

Still, the drought stretched on.

And the gourd beneath the floor continued to fill.

The Bond Between Two Silences

Munei had long believed that grief made one self-ish. That sorrow narrowed the heart into something small, something closed. But Tshilidzi had proved her wrong.

It was in the way he looked at things – truly looked, as if even a leaf might tell a story. It was in the way he asked questions that peeled her open without her realising. 'Did your son have a favourite tree?' 'Do you still dream of his voice?' 'When was the last time you smiled without guilt?'

No one had ever asked her such things. And so, slowly, she told him. About Vhutshilo and his bad jokes. About Tenda's first word being 'mud'. About how she used to dance with her feet in the stream while cooking. Tshilidzi listened like someone storing every syllable in a sacred place.

One evening, while stirring porridge, Munei asked, 'Why do you never ask about the gourd?'

He blinked, surprised. 'I thought it was your heart.'

She laughed for the first time in years – a short, soft burst that startled them both.

'It is,' she said.

From then on, they did everything together. They planted beans even though the soil cracked beneath them. They read the old book of proverbs left by her grandmother. They painted the inside of the hut with handprints and symbols from Tshilidzi's dreams. And when the wind howled too loudly at night, they sat close, wrapped in the shawl that once held Munei's hope.

The villagers began to notice. They saw the boy walking with Munei to the old well, saw her smiling at children again. Rumours softened into wonder. Some brought gifts. Others left letters at her doorstep, asking for healing, prayers, anything. Munei was changing, and so was the boy.

Beneath the Marula Tree (A Flicker in the Dark)

One morning, Tshilidzi awoke burning with fever. It came suddenly, as if the earth had tried to smother him in heat. His breaths were short, shallow. His hands trembled. Munei's old panic returned – her limbs remembering how it felt to hold a dying child. She ground herbs with trembling fingers, placed cold cloths on his chest, sang songs of calling and protection. But the fever laughed at her efforts.

'Don't take him too,' she begged the shadows. 'Don't take this one.'

She went to the gourd. For years she had kept it hidden – her private ocean of grief. Now, desperate, she uncovered the floor, lifted it into her arms and opened the lid.

And something happened.

The wind stopped.

The fire dimmed.

The gourd was no longer filled with water.

It was glowing.

Not brightly. Not violently. But steadily. A gentle pulse of light and warmth – like breath. Munei placed her hand inside, and a voice – not spoken but felt – rushed through her.

'You have mourned enough. Now release.'

She touched Tshilidzi's forehead. He stilled. Then, slowly, his chest rose with ease. His skin cooled. His eyelids fluttered. He looked at her.

'I saw them,' he whispered. 'Your son, your husband. They said to tell you . . . the rain remembers.'

The Gourd of Tears

The next morning, Tshilidzi saw the glint of the gourd's polished neck, half-buried beneath the clay floor. He pulled it out carefully, hands steady. When Munei returned, she found him sitting by the fire, holding it. She froze.

'You weren't meant to touch that,' she whispered, voice trembling.

'I didn't break it,' he said, placing it gently on the mat between them. 'But it's full.'

They both looked at it. The gourd that held every tear she had shed for fourteen years. The last water she had known. It sloshed softly, like a memory trying to wake.

Munei sat down, more slowly than usual, as if the air had thickened.

'I thought … if I saved every drop I cried … one day, I could give it back to the earth.'

Stirring the Earth (The Rain Returns)

That night, clouds gathered for the first time in a decade. The wind shifted, carrying not dust but the smell of coming change. Animals stirred. Children pointed. Elders held their breath.

And then it came.

Not a storm. Not a flood. But a gentle, steady rain. It fell on rooftops, on tin buckets, on dry bones of trees. It soaked the earth, filled the wells, sang against every surface. Munei stepped outside, arms outstretched. The shawl slipped from her shoulders and was soaked through in seconds. She turned to Tshilidzi, who was laughing, dancing barefoot in the mud.

'You did it,' he shouted. 'You opened your heart!'

But she shook her head.

'No. We did it together.'

The villagers came in waves. They dropped to their knees. They cried. They praised. They touched Munei's feet and Tshilidzi's hands. And in the middle of it all, the gourd – still glowing – sat quietly at her doorway, overflowing not with water, but with the stories of all she had lost . . . and all she had found again.

A Change in the Wind

The following days were filled with life. The crops began to grow again, slowly but steadily, and the village flourished in a way it hadn't in years. The women sang as they worked in the fields, their voices rising to meet the sky. The men returned to their work, their hearts lighter than they had been in years. The children played, their laughter filling the air once more.

But Munei was different now. No longer the widow who had buried rain, she had become the woman who had called it back. Her garden, once dry and barren, bloomed with life. The marula tree her husband had planted all those years ago began to show signs of new growth, its branches reaching towards the sky as if in gratitude for the rain that had returned.

Munei no longer spent her night alone by the fire, wrapped in a shawl that once held only her grief.

Now, Tshilidzi sat with her, and they shared stories, dreams and moments of quiet companionship. The villagers began to see her differently too. No longer a woman cursed by the loss of her loved ones, but a woman who had found her way back to life. They no longer feared her, instead they sought her wisdom, her strength and her quiet resilience.

Munei knew that she had buried rain once, but now, she had learned to let it flow. The world around her had changed, and in the quiet moment of the evening, with the wind in her hair and the earth beneath her feet, Munei realised her own heart had shifted too. She was no longer waiting for the rain to fall. She had learned to make it come.

The Legacy

Years passed. Tshilidzi grew tall, strong. Wise beyond his age. He learned the names of all the herbs. Learned the rhythm of the soil. Learned how to listen, not just to people, but to the wind, to fire, to silence.

Munei grew old. But not bitter. She laughed often now. Cooked too much. Told stories to every child who visited. When she passed, she was wrapped in her shawl, her gourd beside her. The villagers buried her beneath the marula tree, which bloomed for the first time since Vhutshilo had planted it.

Tshilidzi stayed. He became the new keeper of stories; he taught children how to cry and still be strong. He taught them to plant, even during droughts.

The Boy Who Remembers Rain

Years passed and Dzimauli began to flourish again, though not in the way people expected. Life slowly returned to the village, but it was different now, tinged with something deeper, something learned through loss and love.

Tshilidzi, now a young man, sat under the marula tree, the same tree Munei's husband Vhutshilo had planted many years ago. The branches were heavy with fruit, and the soil around its base, once dry and cracked, was now rich and dark. Life had found its way back, in small ways, through the perseverance of people like Munei and Tshilidzi.

He held a gourd in his hands, not one of grief this time, but of memory. It was worn and weathered, its surface smooth from years of holding water, stories and hopes. The stories were no longer just Munei's; they were his now, carried forward with every passing year.

The children ran and played nearby, their laughter echoing through the air. They had never known the true weight of silence, of a land without rain, of the grief that once hung thick over Dzimauli. To them, rain was a blessing, a gift that came without question.

But Tshilidzi knew.

Now grown, Tshilidzi sat under the same tree where he once played. He had his own gourd now. He knew the land had once been barren, both in soil and in spirit. He had lived through it. And so, he told the children the story.

'There was a woman,' he began, his voice steady, carrying through the warm air. 'A woman who buried rain with her tears. She thought she had lost everything – her love, her child, her hope. But she was wrong. She was a seed. And like all seeds, she was waiting for rain.'

The children gathered around him, their faces full of wonder, not understanding fully, but feeling the weight of the words.

'Why rain?' one of the younger boys asked.

Tshilidzi smiled softly, the corners of his mouth lifting just slightly. 'Because rain gives life. It nourishes the earth, just like love nourishes the heart. Without it, there can be no growth, no change. And the woman knew that. She knew that even in the darkest times, the rain was waiting to return. It just needed to be called.'

He paused, looking up at the sky, which was slowly gathering clouds. A breeze stirred, gentle, like a memory from the past. The children followed his gaze, eyes wide as they saw the change in the air.

'The rain listens,' he continued, his voice almost a whisper now. 'But it answers to love. And love always finds its way, even in the hardest times. That's what the woman taught me, and that's what I will teach you.'

He looked down at the gourd in his hands, his fingers tracing the edges. 'When Munei passed, she left me with these words, and this story. She said that one day, when I was old enough, I would tell it to others. And so, I do. I tell you this story, so you never forget what she gave us.'

Tshilidzi stood up, the gourd tucked carefully into his arms and looked out over the village. The rain had started, slow at first, just a few drops that kissed the dry earth. But soon, it would pour, filling the rivers, the wells and the hearts of those who had forgotten how much they had been waiting for it.

The children ran out into the rain, their laughter blending with the sound of the storm. Tshilidzi stood still, watching them, feeling the weight of history behind him and the promise of the future ahead. He could hear Munei's voice in the back of his mind, as clearly as if she were standing right beside him: 'The rain remembers'.

And he knew, as he always would, that the story of the woman who buried rain would never be forgotten. And when they ask him if the story is true, he smiles.

Then he points to the sky, where clouds gather gently.

And he whispers, 'Ask the rain.'

NO GOOD DEED
JACQUI AIRES

FINALLY, AN AUCTIONEER'S GAVEL bashed open their new front door, in a manner of speaking, and Phil and Tilda Hope entered. She, for the first time. He'd been there a few times before. Scoped the place.

'Baby, *this* is how you acquire a home,' he said. 'Find a sagging suburb, an owner to match, and when it falls apart – pounce!' A house on Zonnebloem Str. Voetstoots. Everything as is. Personal effects removed. Furniture and fixtures included, and the odd appliance orphaned by the sheriff.

Tilda opened the fridge first – it seemed innocuous but she had to check. The pong of sour milk whacked her nostrils. 'Ew!' Phil shrugged. 'Sorry, I thought I'd thrown that away. There's an element of risk – with this kind of purchase.'

'Oh look, a welcome gift,' she said, as her husband scrambled to get rid of half-used Skip washing powder and some crooked hangers in the laundry room.

'Tildy – I swear, someone's playing a silly trick.' In the spare room: potent citronella. 'Now *this* I put here on purpose', he said, 'to repel flies and mozzies.'

Next, the lounge. Behind a cornflower-blue couch, tawny stains leapt out, as if coffee had been thrown against the wall. Not the expensive kind, the vicious kind. A hysterical spillage, no doubt. Some low-class violence. She glared at him.

'We – I – *did* paint inside. There'll be hell to pay.' He tussled in his pocket for a hanky to wipe it off with, cursing invisible culprits.

She went into the dining room next. It had a ten-seater, which had been specified as 'unused' in the brochure. 'We'll replace *these* ugly bits', she said, gesturing at the chairs covered in scarlet velveteen, 'but the table can stay. Can't easily find such quality. Not this size.'

'A bargain,' he confirmed.

He guided her to the patio doors.

Scraps of rust flittered like dandruff as he rattled them open. 'Bit of putty will do the trick.' Behold: a kidney-shaped pool. Slasto paving. Weed-snuffed flowerbeds. She inhaled her luck. Jacarandas bordered their new address, along the boundary wall. Triumph.

'Incredibly quiet,' he said, 'considering the main road is a stone's throw. No one will know we're here.'

Dead bees crunched underfoot as she patrolled the garden, perhaps drunk on the mimosifolia – pretty lilac flecks patterning the ground.

'Invasive species,' he said, reading her mind, admiring their beauty nonetheless. 'Worth it for the month they flower.' They stood awhile, contemplating thirsty trees sucking up more than their fair share, and stared at the still water, apprehensive about its greenish hue. She bent over to take a closer look, to no reflection at all.

'A bit cloudy. Where's the HTH?'

'Oh, that won't do, Tildy. The pump's off. Loadshedding and whatnot.'

'We'll need solar then,' she replied, cataloguing work to be done. She looked up at the house from the vantage point of the slope gradating downwards, so that it appeared bigger than it was, and less scruffy. A hole in the razor wire needed repair. Erf size, 940 square metres. Too much property, not enough under-roof – a fitting metaphor for the country, she thought. For them.

'Let's go inside,' he directed her.

A trail of ants guided them back over the threshold, through the side door, a short-cut via the pantry, down the corridor, and back into the lounge, to the cornflower-blue couch, askew from the wall where the stains still languished.

He patted the scrunched-up hanky stuffed in his pocket. 'I guess it didn't come off as well as I'd thought.' She agreed – a very stubborn mark.

'The domestic starts on Tuesday,' she chortled. 'Handy Andy will sort it,' he added, 'ha-ha.' She scratched her legs. They were itchy. Little red dots appeared. A rash, it seemed.

'Oh my, Tildy –'

'Dammit! Is there calamine lotion?' Tingling scurried up her shins and knees, and settled into her inner thighs, like she was waist-deep in nettles. She dug her nails into her stockings to get at the skin underneath. Eina! Phil looked politely away, picking up his liquorice-black briefcase. Not real leather. Not a bit.

'I should warn you, Tildy –'

'Just go, Phil, or you'll be late. I'll investigate the rest myself,' she cheerily urged, eager to peel off her blouse right there as hot lava spread across her back. Fleas – scabies? He groped futilely for a set of keys at the garden gate. 'I can see from here that it's only a latch,' she called out. 'You ought to know.'

He chuckled embarrassedly. 'Oh, ja. Forgot.'

He flipped open the little iron hinge, clipping it behind him. On the pavement he looked up and down the street, as if searching for someone. 'Go!' she willed.

He sped off in a faded yellow Volksie, if one could call that speeding. It spluttered and jerked, choking for air.

She whipped 'round to hunt for ice, to relieve manifest pustules. The front entrance wasn't as charming in her current mood. Two flourishing rose bushes flanked the stoep, ivory petals she recalled, from the ad. Not feeling well enough to examine them properly now, she raced past dead, withered vines in bone-dry soil, itchiness covering her whole body like a scratchy winter blanket.

* * *

When the man arrived back at 5 pm, he found his wife beside herself. 'The roses . . . '

'Never mind the roses, you're allergic anyway. I've brought you something for your rash. All will be okay!' He pecked her on the cheek and looked around their abode. 'Finally! A good scrub. A lick of paint. Then it's good to go. I know you're up to it! Let's celebrate!' He handed her a tin of sugary fizz and jived in the lounge.

'You're delirious, Phil.'

'I am, Tildy! Wholesale bliss! Check that sapphire colour out there! Makes the place special, eh? Super-lux!'

She joined him at the window, through which the pool seemed almost blue, turning periwinkle, then violet, the sunset-sky a landscape of pastel-streaked dreams. 'I'd better learn to swim. Otherwise . . . '

'One day I'll teach you,' he said. 'For now, dip your toes in! Maybe up to the knees – no going under. Keep your head above water, at all times.'

'We could drain it? Fill it with concrete. Pave over it. Make a second patio . . .'

'I will not! Who is this crazy woman, eh, suggesting such things – when we chose this house for exactly that! Fence, lawn, pool, tree. Picture-perfect.'

'Did we? Choose it? I feel as if maybe . . . that agent. What's his name? Squeezing himself between us so rudely. Such a pushy character. He didn't seem right in the head. Looked familiar though – can't place why.'

'Him? Pay no attention. It's how things are done. We caught a break, well-deserved. A bond! I mean, unheard of! On our salary! Well, mine. For now. You're resting nicely – and you can take all the time you need.' He pulled her in for a hug – 'Our own *home*, Tildy. Our very own. And d'ya know what this calls for? Music! Let's dance!'

He whistled and hummed, tapped his feet, clapped his hands, ta-da-ta-di-ta-do-ta-da, brrrrrbmmmf, ta-ta-ta-ta-tee-tee-tee, pretending a coherent tune, something one might hear on the radio, and twirled her like a Catherine wheel, singing to 'Home Sweet Home!' – while in the corner, a shadowy coil went unnoticed, slithering out of sight by the time they spun in its direction.

'Careful, you'll dislocate a joint, you dancing queen . . .'

'Oh no, Til, I'm *relocating* you!' he laughed, and waltzed them down the shabby corridor into the kitchen, where old stove plates sat like fried eggs on a laminate countertop, next to an empty bread bin. They heard the pitter-patter of rat feet in the pantry, which imaginary saxophones and vocals could not muffle – so he swung to the side with her in tow, to flick on the dusty light bulb.

'*Fok!*'

Not rats. A colony of cockroaches instead, busybodies, rummaging and shivering on the tiles, oblivious to hopes barely articulated on the title deed. 'Man, grab some Doom!'

She dug inside a tatty little box marked 'rest of kitchen stuff' and retrieved a half-empty can of poison. He sprayed until his eyes watered and his throat hurt. 'It's a fixer-upper,' he coughed, scooping carcasses into the trash. 'I never said any different.'

'You never said at all.'

She squirted waterfalls of bleach to cleanse the massacre, furious fingers squeezing and squeezing, until the last drop. 'That good-for-nothing agent, what a dud! He said it was a gem of a place. More like germ. Someone else's hangers, vrot milk, filthy marks on the wall – the pool is *green* – what a spectacle.'

'*Our* spectacle. On the positive side, the light worked. That's a nice surprise, eh?'

'No, I mean it.'

'People aren't easily erased, Til. But it's legit. Letterheads, fine print. The conveyancer's stamp. A councilman's signature. The Master's date, stamp and signature. A lot of hands involved, lots of layers. Bona fide. Hereto, notwithstanding. Domicilium citandi et executandi. The whole nine yards.'

She stood in the half-dark, in the thick, gross atmosphere, consoling herself with imagined happiness for a quiet minute. She'd hoped this house would feel new, but already, she intuited a grave intrusion. When she'd hesitated about going through with it, Phil had said: 'We're bystanders, Tildy. Nothing to do with us. Am I a fancy shmancy investor? Or mister-nobody Phil, stapling papers in that rubbish office, eh?'

She laughed – 'Ja, okay. It's not our fault. We're not the bank. We just take our chances where we can.' She draped a couple of worn sheets across the windowpanes, locked the doors – not so much locking as barricading – and, eventually, intimacy sucked them to sleep.

When they woke, it was already Monday, whereupon Phil put on his supervisor shirt to start his new promotion – same swivel chair, same office, but upgraded to red-pen, a role with no consequence and wages to match. Yet, proud, tucked and belted, he set off vigorously – with a wave, a peck, and a 'have-a-nice-day' – and the lady phoned pest control from a list of recommended contacts.

* * *

Fortuin's Maintenance pulled up at 9 am. The driver got out, breezed through the gate, and walked up the garden path toward her, in blue overalls and cap – a lazy eye, wide grin, an almost-limp, one couldn't be sure if it were injury or mannerism – and she said, 'You again!'

The man was perplexed. 'Meaning?'

When he was close enough, she doubted herself. 'Oh, it's . . . well, you look like . . . are you related to . . . ?' He stared, whether from imbecility or menace, she couldn't tell. 'You resemble someone', she clarified.

'Are you saying we all look alike?'

'No!' she replied in horror.

'Relax. I'm joking. If you've seen one blue overall, you've seen them all, ne.' And he winked, a sparkle in his eye. 'So, what problem are we solving today, ma'am?'

'As I said, pests. Rats, ants, cockroaches – the trifecta! Disgusting.'

'All God's creatures,' he chuckled.

'The devil's, you mean.'

'Matter of perspective. Crickets?'

'I don't know about that. You're here for rats.'

They walked around the back and he seemed to know the way – or if he didn't, he was unintimidated.

'We heard them first in the pantry, and then in every room', she described, 'as if they were following us through the walls – all night. I didn't sleep, and I feel quite ill.'

'If they were in the pantry – it's the food. Obviously.'

'No, we've only just moved in.'

They stepped over the threshold, through a side door, into the pantry – and the lady froze. Stupefied. In front of her: tinned beans, tinned sweetcorn, tinned peas, *Marie* biscuits! Rolls of them, side by side. Pilchards. Chakalaka. Bovril. A saucer with half-eaten Provita. Dumbstruck, her mouth formed a round, hollow O – like a guppy fish.

'See here's the culprit, ma'am,' he said. 'Check.' The man picked up a chunk of bread, chewed with spittle. 'Shh, listen,' he whispered. Pitter-patter, pitter-patter, pitter-patter. She shuddered. They were overhead.

'They sound . . . huge,' she said, with dread.

'Like little children. Like kids running around, playing.' He grinned. 'Pitter-patter, pitter-patter . . . ' he mimicked, running in mini-circles, 'pitter-patter, pitter-patter,' making the lady dizzy and queasy and nauseous – and she felt a jiggling in her intestines, wriggly worms gyrating in there, rearranging her manners, bequeathing an imminent and unfathomable sickness. She vomited in the kitchen sink – with no time for shame to intercede. The man's only reaction was to retrieve resources from his bakkie, so she excused herself to lie down.

She couldn't be sure when he left, or when she woke, legs twisted, afternoon shadows like wallpapers of despair, mouth dry, disoriented. She got up. The pool was blue-green in the twilight, the kreepy-krauly an unmoving blob.

And then the crickets started.

First, just one. A friendly-sounding *chirrup*. A not unpleasant memory, along with frogs in childhood, which the hadedas have since gobbled, and shongololos too, and lizards.

Well, they're gone. The happy times. It's screeching demons that remain. And Phil. There are garden crickets and house crickets, that much she knew – the latter being small and beige, almost microscopic – undetectable actually, only a shrill torture in your inner ear. She flung her hands over her head to shut it off – a high-pitch high-frequency ringing, like a demented alarm clock, like squealing pigs. When this couldn't block it out, she found tape and bandages – and by the time Phil walked through the door, at 6:30 pm (supervisor's time) he saw a mummy rocking back-and-forth on the bedroom floor.

'Good god, Tilda!' He laughed, bending down to kiss his wife hello. 'Say what now? Crickets? Can't hear a thing! Not at all! – look at you – okay, calm down – don't stress – I'll scavenge noise-cancelling thingies.'

He gently removed the debris from her head and ran her a hot bath – the first and last – and added a cup of Radox, so she could hide in the bubbles and recover.

'Tildy, it was a Checkers delivery,' he explained from the bedroom, getting into pyjamas. 'Payday. We'd said, let's fill up so you don't have to leave the house. The fridge is chock-full too. We'd said – stuff those zombies out there, we'll buy everything in one go. So you can rest.' She had no recollection. Couldn't locate that conversation – couldn't locate the groceries offloaded, shuffled and organised.

'In any event, Tildy, you do remember the visitors?' He came in with a towel for her, 'Or is there a void in there?' he said, tapping her skull.

'Yes, Phil. A dinner party, and I'm to make tripe curry.'

'My best! Jelly and custard for dessert – and I don't care if they think that's funny. No airs and graces here.'

* * *

At 11 am, ValWater Pool Services arrived. A man with a gammy leg and a glass eye shuffled to the front door and buzzed. She opened –

'You?!'

'I beg yours, ma'am? Pool repair.'

Before she could query, he traipsed through the house, flung open the patio doors, sending rust into the ether like confetti, and whistled loudly. 'This thing is kaput!'

'No kidding. It's radioactive green. A pipe is loose, I can't lift the lid on the filter, it's soldered shut with gunk. Our agent said –'

'Eish, Mrs – can't trust them.'

'So, what do we do?'

'We klap this algae dead!' he chuckled. 'Carry on with your day, ma'am. I'll tinker.'

* * *

'Phil, that degenerate was here for *ages*. Now we've got two invoices to pay. The pests and the pool. And I don't think either is fixed!'

She was pacing up and down the lounge, arms flailing, with headphones on, the noise-cancelling ones he brought home – because she said the demons were screeching, but he has tinnitus anyway and can't hear crickets – 'And Dolly Cleaners didn't dispatch *anyone* despite numerous calls and numerous arrangements, so this stain here –' she said, pointing violently at the wall behind the couch, 'and that stain *there* –' she said, showing him a purple bruise on the carpet, whether grapejuice, wine, gravy, or something else, she didn't want to know what, 'never-mind the *mould* I'm starting to see –'

He shot into action to soothe his wife, flinging on an imaginary record, so the trumpets could lift her spirits. Brrrrrrmppfffff . . . he trilled, fingers twiddling fresh air like a maestro. 'Get the plumbers in, Tildy, to check,' he sang between pursed lips. 'It's teething, that's all. Home ownership, eh!'

'Whose home?'

'What d'you mean who's home? We're home!'

* * *

Pitter-patter, pitter-patter, pitter-patter. Scratching, scuttling. Her skin crawled. Phil snored. Something was in these walls – not only rats, they had yet to see them. A presence. No, that would imply the present.

A *passance.*

They thought they'd be getting a treasure – the way the agent talked this place up.

'Folks, this house is full of surprises! You won't believe your eyes! *Unimaginable* joy. You'll be entertaining your friends like nothing! Every day, you'll say, we landed our bums in the butter!'

* * *

The meat van pulled up. Corp. O. Real Butchery. The driver got out, blue overalls, Polaroid sunglasses, dragging one foot behind him, a pitiful stride. 'Morning ma'am,' he said, a little too sunnily, flicking up the latch on the garden gate, like he knew just what to do.

'Delivery for Mrs –'

'This way,' she instructed, and he followed her to the deep freezer out back, by the pantry. He slapped the offal down. 'Livers, heart, lungs, kidney, spleen, tongue – *alles*.'

'Thanks, you can leave the receipt there – I've just made a jam sandwich. Would you like half?'

'With our apricots? Very much!' The man took off his *brille* and winked at her, a little sparkle in his eye – and she jumped back in fright. 'Ma'am, you okay? I didn't mean to – it's a twitch, I can't help it. No winking, I promise!' He put the Polaroids back on, but she'd already seen it, the lazy-eye – and now her spine tingled with cold fear.

'What do you want?' she asked, hands behind her back to fumble discreetly for a knife.

'Me? Niks,' he chuckled. 'A second life maybe. Nice house, this. Big garden. But I see it's full of weeds – no gardener?'

'He quit. Look, my husband will be home any second, he's working half-day.'

'How 'bout *I* cut your grass for you, for cheap? I see the land's tugging this way and that.'

'Kind offer, but a garden service has been appointed. You're not wrong, I feel a little – strangled – by the excess.' Oddly, they were transplanted outside, a blip in time she couldn't fill, so he could point out dead fruit, maggot-infested, from an apricot tree she hadn't noticed before.

'Lemme guess, ma'am: Lucky's Landscapers!'

'How'd you know?' the lady asked, her entrails knotting.

The man shrugged. 'I know the area.'

Phil wasn't working half-day – so she acquiesced to chit-chat in her sweetest voice, in terror.

'Rumour has it there's a rare antique in this dwelling-place,' he said, grinning.

'Not to my knowledge,' she replied.

'No? A "credenza" or kist? Or is it a bureau? I forget the difference. Such la-di-da words! Could even be a Chippendale!' he chuckled.

'A who?' – and she attempted to chuckle along with him.

'Can I have a peep?' he asked, stepping right past her, down the corridor to the dining-room – she had no inkling how they transitioned inside. 'Look.' He pointed to a wooden crate in the dining-room, suffocated by dirty clothes, threadbare scatter cushions, other junk and old books. With quick violence, he shoved the whole pile on the floor, to show her. 'Tsk, tsk, madam.' He clicked his tongue.

'So what?' she said, defensively. 'So, we painted over it. Came with the house.' She pointed to a can of left-over paint. Red. 'To match the marvellous lamp, *dahling!* I was bored. Sue me.'

He threw up his hands in mock defeat – 'Well, in that case, *bon courage* for what lies ahead.'

'Sterkte,' she matched, aiming at humour.

His face darkened. 'Vasssssbyt', he hissed.

Then he chuckled. 'Bambelela madam – much indebted, much obliged – and that's me done for the day – and by the way, that's a helluva leak you've got in the roof.' He rolled his eyes upwards like a madman – and disappeared.

* * *

'We're locked in, Til. We signed on the dotted line. What's Latin for "locked in"? Enforceable, that's what. There's no getting out of this.'

The couple sat on the front stoep as night fell, facing the street, on plastic stools, using an upturned bin for a table. He'd installed a thick padlock on the gate – and they were doing sums.

Inside, three buckets caught dripping water, the couch soaked and ruined. He tapped assets and liabilities on his little calculator, and she scribbled the figures down.

'And insurance won't budge?' he asked, shuffling through quotes for waterproofing.

'They said "wear and tear" to everything, Phil. They said, "Calm down, Mrs – you mustn't insult the personnel.

Your policy has exclusions." I asked for an assessor; they cut me off. When I called back, it said: "This number does not exist."'

'They know how to screw the underdog, eh. Take, take, take.'

'Plus, I wasn't as convincing as I could've been, Phil. Read out the correct details – spoke with confidence – but airtime ran out. Amateur.'

He scratched his head, hoping to pluck a solution, settling instead on stargazing. 'Just the one little twinkle up there,' he pointed. 'Hardly heaven, but it's still a sign. We're not alone.'

'That's a plane, Phil. And you know what else he said? – he said, "Careful this thing doesn't liquidate you." What thing, I asked. He sneered and vanished – as if I'd conjured it! Phil, I thought to myself: that's it, Tilda, now you've *really* lost the plot. Bad energy *oozed* out of that half-wit, Phil. What a cheek! Had a go at me about repainting that wooden box thing. I mean, it's *our* house! Isn't it?'

'Yes, but Tildy – I have to ask: when I came home, you'd left all the taps running, bath and kitchen, and that's a waste. A frightful waste. You haven't … you know … had a little accident, a little relapse? The microwave's been smashed to smithereens.'

'It's a process, Phil. Some days are better than others. And who's to say it was me?'

* * *

She pulled a tarp across the pool, with great difficulty. Desuetude ate the marbelite. Despite Phil's overtime, they couldn't ever have afforded to fix the filter, pump or kreepy – none of it. They had to triage. Burst pipes were gutting the house, and rising damp had afflicted most of the rooms, spoiling walls, rotting skirting boards – releasing spores.

The air was unsanitary.

In the spare room, an abandoned teddy bear was so sodden as to be relieved of its stuffing. She didn't dare go in there – it echoed a child's laughter, and she ached to hear it. Phil said, 'Tildy, that's the house next door. Take your pills.'

* * *

'Defaulting on these repairs will compound the ground-swell,' the plumber advised. Called in from the same list of contacts. 'Foundation's unstable.'

'So *much* damage, I don't understand?' The man agreed it was unaccountable. That he too, took pity at the plight of the place. How much it seeped – 'enough to drown a person' he emphasised, glancing at the covered pool through the bedroom window, which always let in peculiar shades of light, never matching the weather outside. He gave her the creeps. He had an eye-patch and a pulled leg-muscle – he said, 'Don't laugh. I've been in the wars.'

'Stagnant water. Evaporating slowly,' she replied. 'A swamp! Never even had the chance to lie out there on a deckchair. Between that and the stench from the drains –'

' – A crime-scene,' he joked.

'Home ownership has its challenges. Cost of living crisis. Will you manage, then – up there on the roof? That ladder of yours looks awfully rickety.'

'Lady, credit where credit is due! Sof.T. Plumbing & Electrical is nothing if not die-hard!'

'You sound just like my husband, works 'till he drops – I'll get you a glass of Oros. It's a messy job, this. A refreshment will help.'

'Ma'am, I will appreciate.'

* * *

'We'll make adjustments, that's all.' They'd been forced into the dining room, with no dinner parties to speak of. Termites had become a menace. 'Watch out – these bastards tunnel and hollow-out,' the guy had said. A wretched man he was, Phil, hopping on one leg, with pink-eye. The invoice was ludicrous.

They sat at opposite ends of the table, facing each other, eight empty seats in between, cosplaying a banquet. It was candlelight and cold suppers to boot – a power-surge having fizzled all the mod cons.

'Don't worry, Tildy. At month-end, we get in new guys – and they fix everything! One shot! Done! New overdraft! A loan for a loan. Demons too. We poison the life outta here! Promise.'

Screeching crickets meant she had to wear headphones from sunset – even sleep with them on, which she tried, but couldn't. Insomnia-ridden, she hunted at night, begging the site of infestation to reveal itself. Phil was humouring her – in truth, he heard nothing. He said, 'Til, remember the doctor's orders. Self-care.'

Under the paint, the kist complained, making her hair stand. 'Self-care, my foot.'

'Yes, Til, it creaks. Wood expands and contracts. It's a handmade thing. It's got some life to it. We'll make the house work. You'll see.' There was a mark on his supervisor shirt – but she didn't say anything. When last had laundry been done? Come to think of it, never.

'Phil, we've tampered with the wrong thing.'

* * *

They were on the stoep again, backs against the pitch-dark inside – facing the street and the other houses, whose lights were blinking happily. He'd looped an additional chain on the gate.

'Credenza, cadenza. Who cares, man. It's junk. And if that weirdo comes here again –'

'They're *all* weird. You haven't met these reprobates – I deal with them day in, day out. Carbon copies, the lot of them. Coming and going like they own the place! And they've repaired bugger-all. We're haemorrhaging money, Phil. I'm scared. This place . . . I feel it's against us.'

'It *is* against us! And will be for thirty years – at least. With interest! Everything is against us – us strugglers. No overtime, no lights. No twelve-hour shifts, no nothing. No sun-up to sun-down – no nada! Look, I'm working my backside off here. When do I get time for depression? Maybe we swop, eh – I take a depression holiday, you work the control room. How's that?'

'You're a real comedian now – you know I'd work in a heartbeat. If you'd let me.'

'Til, you have to stand guard, you hear? I can't have you running off the property – it leaves us exposed.'

* * *

'Yoo-hoo!' the neighbour called over the gate. A committee-looking type of woman, dressed like a Queenspark mannequin. 'Mrs –'

Tilda hid by the freezer out back, crouching silently. Phil had said, 'From now on, don't answer. Not for anyone. For any reason. Stay inside. We can't be served if we can't be found.'

'You okay in there? I heard noises last night. Terrible noises. I know something's not right! I want to help. Hello? I nearly called the police. Must I? Mrs – ?'

Queenspark lady rattled the chain. Then she threw her hands up and stormed off. Third time this neighbour's come to interfere. Where Tilda hid, brown fluid had congealed on the floor, and lo, there lay the agent's card. Finally! She picked it up. He needed to come back here and settle, once and for all – why did he lie. There was nothing to show for what they had paid.

But first, to keep her marriage in the balance, she faced the laundry room head-on. A generator was on loan from Phil's boss. The Skip was still there – no surprise – and those hangers. She stuffed a load into the machine – it took all her effort, the mundanity. Say she *did* get a job – say Phil caved. What would it be? What should she propose?

She pressed 'Start', and went for a lie-down, diesel fumes and washing powder having conspired to give her a skull-splitting headache.

* * *

'Oh, Tildy. What's happened here?' It was Phil in the dark. She sat up, drowsy. 'Gosh, I don't know – I only wanted a short nap.' It was past 10 pm; he'd been working late.

'The house is a wreck.'

'No more than usual. I did the washing – did you see? We'll have clean clothes for a change.'

He gestured for her to follow him out the bedroom, to the laundry to see for herself. He'd pulled it out the machine for hanging up – but that wasn't going to be possible. The load was botched. Their clothes ribboned – in tatters. The fabric spun out – disintegrated. Seams undone. Threads unpicked. Fish moths lay strewn in clumps of linen and cotton and polyester.

'Phil, we're under attack. I didn't do this.'

The man slumped to the floor like a sack of potatoes, and she beside him. 'How long have we been here, Til?'

'I don't know. I've lost track. Did we imagine the deal? Where's our file? Feels like forever.'

They sat in silence, cockroaches skipping, darting and breeding all around them.

* * *

'You can't hide forever in there! I'm calling the police, Mrs –'

Tilda peeped out of moth-bitten sheets-for-curtains, to watch the woman rattling the chain again.

'Please speak to me! We need to talk! We're all affected!'

This time, the neighbour wasn't giving up, that much was clear. So Tilda wrapped her housecoat tight around her and opened the front door.

'I'm coming.'

She saw the woman's expression as she walked out – knew to expect it – because her appearance had deteriorated.

'Mrs – are you okay? The racket from your place! There's concern, you see, about – oh, let me not beat around the bush. This house is an unmitigated eyesore! I'm sorry, it sounds harsh. But it's true.'

'No, I understand,' Tilda whispered hoarsely. 'We're battling the elements, I'm afraid – but we've committed to all sorts of improvements. Haven't you seen how many contractors come and go, for repairs. We're levelling up.'

'Contractors? We? Who's "we"?'

'Tilers, gutter rehabilitation – they're here nearly every other day. Lucky's, Fortuin's – you must have seen?'

'Dearie – this house is practically abandoned. Windows haven't opened since the last family left. Look how high these weeds are. Lights always off. We hardly realised it had been sold. In fact, has it been? The board is still on the pavement. Says it's going on auction.'

Tilda couldn't see the board behind the wall and was too frightened to look.

'I'm calling the police. There's something rotten in Denmark – don't think I'm stupid.'

'In where? It's just that the agent –'

'Agent of destruction more like. Give me his name. *I* will contact him – if it's a him.'

Tilda retrieved the card from her pocket, the one found by the freezer – gold lettering set against ivory, with the slogan 'People First'. A name was printed on the back, alongside a judicious-looking logo, hiding under a smear of old blood. Mr Good. She handed it over.

The neighbour stared at her, wide-eyed. 'Are you pulling my leg, Mrs – ? "Mr Good?" Listen dearie,' the woman chastised, 'nobody's been to this house, you're fibbing. No repairmen – no one. I live across the way. My veranda faces this direction. I can see the whole front part.'

Tilda's housecoat came undone and flapped in the wind – but she was stricken and unable to fasten it. The neighbour, out of pity, stepped forward and tied it for her – and continued:

'Mrs – you're perturbed, naturally. Who in their right mind could settle here. They suffered, you know. Went under. I felt sorry. Really, I did. One day, your whole life's ahead of you. The next, mad and broke. One affliction, one unfortunate event. And it's all gone. Makes you think.'

'Um, I –'

' – Apparently their stuff's still in there. Don't know how you bear it. Would give me the chills. He – the father, the husband – had a repair company. Rumour has it, he can still be seen up and down this street – I'd

watch out if I were you. If you believe in ghosts! I mean –
the guy went nuts. Lost a child – stillborn, which they
found in a *kist*. Imagine! Laid to rest there – the things
people do in grief. Wife was sectioned – you look a bit
like her, no offence – and he shot himself twice. In the
shin, and then fatally, through the eye. Splat. Brains
everywhere. I wonder if anyone cleaned up? Died intes-
tate. Grisly stuff –'

Tilda let out a cry.

'Oh dearie, I know, I know. So sad. When the sheriff,
or "agent" as you so euphemistically refer to him – nasty
man – disappeared, there was talk the Hopes had something to do with it. He was never found, you know. But
you have his card. Very curious.'

Tilda turned and fled back into the house. She slammed
the door, petrified. Oh, they were in deep trouble now. It
was a long, agonising wait for Phil – and as soon as he
returned, she shrieked – 'The demons! It's punishment!
There's no deed! He wants us gone! It's *his* house!'

'Tildy, calm down. I've sorted things – thank me
later. First, I need this', he said, sliding off her wedding
ring, 'to pawn. I found another one – another crooked
so-and-so. He'll make a file. I swear this time, no more
pavements. No more parks. I want a roof over my head,
for good. And a paper that says so. A proper bloody
document. And I don't care who, but somebody better
stamp it! Now, since no one knows where Sheriff Good

has "retired" to – his deputy's going to fix it. Same price. Here – look. We carry on as the Hopes.'

'We can't! We need new IDs! You have to believe me! The neighbour – she told me things. It's cursed!'

'Now *you're* the real comedian. Tildy, please –'

'The foreclosure. There was more to it.' She pointed to the freezer. 'He's in there.'

'Then who propositioned us, eh?'

'*A ghost!*'

'Tilda – fetch the noise-cancelling thingies. Or let me play you a tune – then you can rest nicely.' Ta-de-ta-da-tra-la-tra-la, brrrrrmpfffff! 'Tomorrow is another day – and, baby, I am going to prune me some roses.'

* * *

The neighbour across the street sat on her veranda, with her favourite rusks and coffee, taking in a sunny, bright morning and the shenanigans of her surrounds. A taxi hit a pothole and the wheel almost flew right off; it was funny! The street was a hive of activity again – including that strange man with the funny eye and weird limp, whistling down the road as usual – 'Nulla Bona Maintenance Services' embossed on blue overalls. He winked, a sparkle in his eye.

She gave a friendly wave, put up her feet and flipped open the tabloids. 'Squatters Arrested! Body Of Missing Sheriff Found! Life Sentences! Beware Scam Artists!'

A MORTICIAN'S INSTINCT
KAMVA MAJO

THE BUSINESS OF DEATH never ends.

Mandla glanced at the bedroom door – and there it was.

It had seeped in through the keyhole and under the frame. Death. Impatient. Refusing to wait for him to step out.

The scent struck – sharp and sour, thick with rot.

It had found its way into his house.

His hands stayed still. His breath flattened. He didn't flinch. He didn't move.

Just like always.

Mandla's Mortuary stood in Khayelitsha – twenty-five minutes from his home in Mowbray. He had grown up in Khayelitsha.

The streets there knew the sound of mourning better than music.

Death wasn't a tragedy there – it was routine. Quick. Expected.

That's why he built his business there. Not because it was home, but because death felt normal there.

But he moved to Mowbray, thinking he would be far away from it.

In Mowbray, people watered their lawns. Smiled at strangers in the mornings. Pretended.

Even their mourning appeared organised. Eyes dry. No women hurled to the floor by the weight of grief, wailing from the gut.

They stayed still – crumbling quietly behind closed doors.

Still, he hadn't known real sleep in years. Not here.

Sometimes he wondered how he was still alive.

No – he'd stopped wondering.

He knew now.

It was The Plan.

Not his – *the one given to him.*

Sadistic, maybe. Or too vast for him to comprehend.

It belonged to something greater.

Something he only ever referred to as *The Red Decree.*

It was uncertain. Like everything else in his life.

Don't feel sorry for him.

That's what he would say.

Save your sorrow for those who betray.

For those who break vows made before God.

For those who transgress against love.

Feel sorry for them – not him.

He cursed under his breath and rushed out of the room, stepping over the dried stain beside his bed.

He wasn't supposed to sleep.

But sleep had come anyway – like a mother's embrace.

It rocked him at the worst possible time.

The bed, once as cold as marble, had suddenly felt warm.

Comforting.

He couldn't resist the pull.

He slept like a baby.

A sign *The Red Decree* was moving pieces. Watching.

He had to do his part. That was the pact.

He walked quickly through the dark corridor.

The only thing that made the silence bearable was the television murmuring in the distance.

When he reached the living room, his mind hesitated.

It took a moment to readjust – the space looked wrong. The sofas were gone, dragged into the garage, and some dumped outside.

His work had followed him home.

There it was.

The body.

Laid out on the makeshift embalming table.

It had been easy to replicate – his desk cleared and wiped down. Strong legs. Easy to clean.

Steel meant nothing to *The Red Decree*. All it demanded was order.

One arm dangled limply off the edge. The form was curled slightly, turned away from the television.

The news anchor's voice floated through the static haze. On the screen, bold letters flashed: **DAY 15 OF THE QUARANTINE**

The world had shut down.

But they didn't know.

The pandemic was just a distraction – something to keep them busy while the real plan unfolded.

Death.

Once, he had feared it.

Now he knew better.

It was never in control.

Just a tool.

A language.

The Red Decree spoke through it.

It was methodical.

It wouldn't stop until everything was gone.

But once it was – once he'd left the world clean –

He would be born again.

His parents would return.

And this time, he would grieve properly.

He would cry for them the way he couldn't before.

Before he began the restoration, he moved to the front windows. Carefully.

Even though *The Red Decree* was here to free him, he feared it too – not because it was cruel, but he learned that freedom was rarely given gently.

He peeled the curtain just enough to peek through.

The street was empty.

No children on bicycles. No teenage lovebirds. No joggers.

The distraction is working.

They are terrified of death.

So afraid, they have stopped living just to hide from it.

A red car cruised past.

A reminder.

The Red Decree was watching.

The work must go on.

But first – coffee and whisky.

The concoction had become his crutch. His sacrament.

The Red Decree had given him The Plan months ago.

He had to be steady enough to carry it out.

The whisky burned on its way down his throat, leaving a bitter sting behind.

Then – he was ready.

He moved toward the embalming table, each step deliberate.

One arm still hung loosely off the edge.

He lifted it – gently, slowly.

It felt both heavy and light in his hands.

He folded it across the body's hip.

The deceased was still clothed.

Normally, the body was stripped before preparation, but he couldn't bring himself to take them off.

It felt like too much.

Leaving the clothes on felt like respect.

The last he could offer.

The news hummed in the background.

The pandemic raged on.

Bodies upon bodies were being hauled off by men in protective coveralls.

The world was in a panic.

But not him.

He knew what they didn't.

As much as he found comfort in watching *The Red Decree's* plan unfold, he still had to tend to his part.

He walked to the TV and unplugged it.

The screen went black – and on it, he saw his reflection, distorted.

Then, he saw it – a figure on the sofa.

Startled, he turned.

The body was still on the table. Peaceful. Unmoved.

He turned back to the TV, disturbed by its tricks, and swivelled it to face the wall.

A distraction.

He returned to the embalming table. Switched on the desk lamp he'd mounted on a bar stool.

It cast a sharp, focused light.

He'd also brought in the dining table from the kitchen to lay out his tools.

Everything was in place.

It was time to embalm the deceased.

But really – he wanted to embalm memory.

'Mandla, you need help . . . There's something inside you, something broken.'

In his thirty years as a mortician, Mandla had seen all the cards *The Red Decree* dealt – death. Grief. Silence.

He'd watched grief split families apart – but always from behind the curtain.

Still, there were times he'd drifted out of the embalming room – into the wave of wailing wives, mothers, sisters.

But it was never their cries that moved him.

It was the ones who stood still.

Silent. A little further back.

Usually a man.

No tears. No expression.

He saw them.

He was them.

Standing at his parents' grave at age nine.

After the funeral, he remembered relatives tiptoeing around him.

'He hasn't cried.'

'I thought he'd break down at the grave.'

But he never did.

He had beaten another boy bloody once at school – just for cutting in line outside Ms Ndungane's class.

He almost got expelled, but the principal heard about his tragedy.

He also remembered the day he broke down – completely – while searching for his mother's ring.

He'd found it later, wedged behind the bedroom curtain.

The same ring he would later use to propose to Savannah.

But he never cried for his parents.

Now, as he slid on the gloves, a thought crept in:

Why am I doing this?

Because this is what I was trained to do.

To preserve. To clean. To finish what others can't face.

He turned the body to face upward.

The lips were slightly parted, as though still stunned by life's fragility.

It was the one truth no one escaped – your turn came when you least expected it.

And suddenly, he remembered his first kiss with Savannah.

It happened in front of the Omen Art Gallery on Long Street.

Night had crept in, and the street stirred to life. Groups of guys and girls drifted toward the buzzier end of the block.

Savannah's lips glistened with Vaseline, catching the flicker of the streetlights.

They had been talking about where their second location would be when the urge to kiss her struck Mandla – sudden and overwhelming.

Nervously, he leaned in.

At first, the kiss was clumsy. Awkward.

Then, as if an unspoken rhythm found them, it settled.

And then – he bit her lip.

She yelped and pulled away.

He froze, worried that people passing by had seen his failure.

She took a breath, then smiled. To his relief, she wasn't bleeding.

'Let me teach you', she said softly.

He had closed his eyes then – nervous, uncertain, badly wanting to get it right.

He closed his eyes now, breath unsteady, as he adjusted the metal wires to seal the jaw.

It was a delicate task – but in this moment, it felt like the most violent thing he had ever done.

When he opened his eyes again, his hands were trembling.

The taste in his mouth was sharp. Metallic.

Nothing hurts quite like watching someone you gave your heart to spit lies through the same mouth they used to kiss you with.

What Savannah never knew was that *The Red Decree* had already warned him.

Red.

That was the sign.

At first, he had believed he couldn't accuse her of cheating unless he caught her – with another man, or woman, in their bed.

He later cursed that naivety.

From Vaseline-smeared lips to crimson-painted ones.

The first time she wore red lipstick, she had said she just wanted to try makeup.

'We're grown now,' she'd said.

'There'll be important events – I want to look the part.'

All he could think was: *Whore.*

Of course, he never said it.

Artists were repulsed by control.

But he wasn't controlling. He just had strong suggestions.

He knew that if he pushed too hard, she'd fall into someone else's arms.

So he kept records.

He filled them out every night – details, patterns. *The Red Lipstick Days.*

Eventually, he'd noticed a pattern.

She wore it when he was working – days she knew he wouldn't be around.

Then, the pattern unravelled.

The red appeared on random days. Unexpected days.

He started to wonder: had she read his records?

Was she outsmarting him?

She was becoming something else –

A Savannah he didn't recognise.

She was killing the woman he'd fallen in love with.

To amuse himself, he'd bought her a red dress for their last anniversary.

She hadn't thought much of it – red was for lovers, after all.

Except they weren't. Not anymore.

They were pretending.

She was pretending.

And he was pretending *back*.

He needed to be sure. He needed evidence.

He didn't mind selling the façade of their dead marriage.

Besides – he knew how to make dead things look nice.

It was his job.

Now, he even hated the good memories.

They clung to him like a phantom limb – gone, but always there, aching when he least expected it.

Once, they'd given him hope of how things could be again.

Now they only pulled him deeper into the void.

His gloved hands moved automatically, setting the features with the practised precision of a mortician.

But inside – he was numb.

The second step: close the eyes.

Those eyes – wide, empty – had once belonged to someone.

Now they stared into nothing.

He pressed the lids shut with care.

Somewhere in the noise of his mind, he remembered another pair of eyes.

The way they had held him still, and in them, he'd seen a peace he could never touch.

Eyes that asked questions, even when her mouth didn't.

That was before the darkness came.

They had been strangers back then, riding the same bus from Mowbray every day.

His eyes always found her – drawn to her presence.

She never looked back.

Her gaze was fixed out the window, like she lived in some other world entirely.

Then one day, the universe stepped in.

Savannah had been standing at the bus stop, a sketch pad in her hand, lost in thought.

A homeless woman and a young girl approached, asking for money.

Savannah looked embarrassed – digging through her tote bag, flustered.

'I'm so sorry,' she'd said, shaking her head. 'I don't have anything. No food, nothing.'

He had watched from the sidelines, then stepped forward and opened his lunchbox.

'Here. Take it,' he said quietly.

The woman smiled.

'God bless you, young man.'

The child's eyes lit up as they walked away.

That was when Savannah looked at him – really looked.

Their eyes met. It wasn't a passing glance. She saw something.

Or thought she did.

Something in her shifted.

He remembered thinking: *It worked.*

That kind act – whatever she thought it was – had brought them together.

They talked on the bus that day.

From that moment, they shared more than just rides.

They shared time. Moments. Lives.

He had been hesitant to tell her about his career plans at first.

She'd told him she was an art student, which hadn't surprised him.

She had the whimsical energy of creatives.

A nauseating love for colours.

Later in their marriage, he suspected she had started dreaming of a colourful life – somewhere far from the grey world she shared with him.

It was a small battle every time they furnished the house –

He wanted steel pots.

She wanted ceramic ones shaped like strawberries.

'They'll bring life into our home,' she said, grinning.

He let her buy them.

A part of him enjoyed seeing her thrilled over silly things.

Her reaction to his job had surprised him.

Her eyes lit up.

'Oh my God! I've never met someone who's gonna be a mortician before!' she laughed, slapping his shoulder.

She had entered his world with the fascination people have about things they think will never touch them.

One night, after too much wine, she admitted that it turned her on – him dealing with death so intimately.

But Mandla realised it wasn't death she was drawn to.

It was what he didn't say.

The steadiness. The quiet. The fact that nothing seemed to move him.

She thought it made him powerful. Dangerous. Mysterious.

He let her believe that, too.

But her desire had become suffocating.

And it wasn't just the pots anymore.

The walls were covered in colourful canvases.

Doors painted in pastels.

Suddenly, his actions impacted someone else's mood.

And their actions affected his.

He used to crave belonging – used to mourn his isolation.

But he had grown into freedom.

And now, he'd traded it away for love.

Part of him had longed for the normalcy he saw in others –

A home that smelled of food.

A wife in an apron.

Children clinging to his legs.

People who would mourn him when he died.

A wailing wife.

Grieving children.

So he stayed. Even though it was clear:

The dead were easier to deal with than the living.

Now, as he closed the deceased's eyes, he wished Savannah's had been easier to read.

Not so vast.

Not so shifting.

He would have preferred stillness – something small. Contained. Predictable.

But once, those very eyes had pulled him in – and he'd gone without hesitation.

That had been his mistake.

Love blurred the red flags.

He chose not to see it.

That Savannah had been unfaithful from the very beginning.

The realisation now stung.

As he sealed the second eyelid shut, he felt the tears welling.

With that one act –

He buried the love.

And the lies.

Then, the body's arm jerked – limp and sudden – striking his stomach.

For a moment, everything stopped.

Then slowly, cautiously, he reached for the hand. It was delicate. Pale.

He lifted it and placed it gently across the abdomen. Then did the same with the other.

He stared at the whole body.

His breath caught as his gaze locked on the bullet hole between the eyes.

A sharp pain shot through his chest – but he couldn't look away.

He stumbled back – then broke into a run toward the kitchen.

His stomach twisted violently.

He leaned over the sink and vomited.

A sour taste burned in his mouth.

He wiped it away with the back of his arm, trying to breathe through it.

My body has become weak. But that doesn't mean I'm wrong.

It has nothing to do with The Plan. Weakness does not mean failure.

I'll carry on anyway.

Cold sweat beaded on his forehead.

He wiped it too – but it kept coming.

A constant reminder.

Of what he'd done.

* * *

After embalming a body, Mandla usually stepped away.

The funeral director took it from there, and he moved on to the next corpse.

But there was no funeral director that day. And no manual.

He had to improvise.

He needed to move the body before the smell seeped through the walls.

Before it reached the street.

Before it alarmed Mrs Booysen – who had been leaving baked treats at his doorstep ever since the quarantine began.

They came with handwritten notes:

Stay strong.

You're not alone.

Strange thing to say to a married man.

Maybe she knows something I don't.

He tossed the baked goods in the bin.

Tore the notes without reading past the first line.

Before he took the body bag to the car, he checked the walls.

He knocked softly, then pressed his ear to the cold surface.

Sometimes *The Red Decree* left messages.

He didn't want to miss the last ones.

Instructions mattered.

Precision mattered.

It was a side effect of the work – everything had to be meticulously done.

He knocked again. Nothing.

Once, he had smashed a hammer into the brick, sure he was one knock away from decoding something vital.

He'd cursed the concrete.

If only these walls were wood – maybe I'd hear better.

Then, with practised ease, he lifted the body bag off the table and stumbled toward the garage.

Even with all his training, it felt heavier now.

The garage was cluttered – sofas stacked and scattered – but he navigated his way to the back of the sedan.

He opened the boot.

Lowered the body in carefully.

The thud of the boot closing left his ears ringing.

Then silence.

Thick. Hollow. Final.

He manually opened the garage.

The cold night air hit his face.

It was crisp. Unpolluted.

It whispered to him:

It's time now. Go on.

But then–

'Man-da-la, hey!'

He heard the familiar, botched pronunciation of his name. Her voice.

Mrs Booysen.

She was a distraction – but he couldn't let her know.

If she knew, she'd try to stop him. Or worse, call someone.

They wouldn't understand The Plan.

They'd ruin everything.

The grey-haired woman wobbled toward the fence that separated their yards.

'Don't walk closer, Man-da-la,' she warned. 'You know this pandemic stuff.'

He hadn't been walking toward her.

He fought the urge to rush to his car and drive off – but that would raise suspicion.

She was already prone to being nosy.

He managed a polite smile.

'You should be asleep, Mrs Booysen. It's not safe for you to be outside at night.'

She waved him off with a chuckle, but her face crinkled with a hint of sadness.

'Oh, this pandemic stuff. Keeps us cooped up inside. Must be hard for you, hey? Seeing all that death?'

'Ja,' he said. Short. Controlled.

He didn't tell her he hadn't been at work for days.

She peered at him more intently.

'Must be hard being all alone, Man-da-la. But you're not alone, okay?'

There was a shift in her tone – gentler. Serious.

'I heard on the radio . . . the things lonely people do to themselves, with this quarantine thingy.'

That caught his attention.

'What kind of things?'

She murmured a short prayer under her breath, crossed herself.

'They kill themselves. Let Satan mess with their minds.'

Her eyes met his.

'We're here, Man-da-la. Even with all this pandemic stuff, okay? You hear me?'

He forced a smile. 'Okay.'

Without another word, he climbed into the car and drove away.

As he drove down the N2 – past grey offices, shopping centres and sun-bleached billboards – the road began to loosen.

Mowbray thinned out behind him.

He took the turn onto Spine Road, heading toward Khayelitsha.

Shacks began to lean into each other like they were sharing secrets.

The silence grew.

Have I given *The Red Decree* too much control over me?

How stupid of me.

He slammed his fist against the steering wheel.

The sound cracked through the quiet. His teeth pressed together; a twitch sparked behind his eye.

Something stirred in his body – a feeling he didn't have time to figure out.

Only The Plan mattered now.

He approached the traffic lights several stops away from his destination.

The dim streetlights cast a weak glow over the cracked asphalt.

The traffic light turned red.

Normally, in this part of Cape Town, no one stopped for red lights – especially not late at night.

Stopping meant inviting trouble.

But for him, red was also a sign to go on.

He pressed harder on the accelerator.

The tires of the sedan screeched as they peeled across the empty road.

His grip tightened on the wheel. He passed the street that turned toward the mortuary.

He finally arrived at the landfill site in Khayelitsha, near the cemetery.

Before him lay the waste of a thousand lives –

Discarded plastics.

Broken dreams.

Remnants of the city's daily churn.

All piled in chaotic heaps.

He parked the car near the edge of the site.

The only light came from the cold, bright moon and the distant glow of street lamps.

The mounds of garbage rose before him – dark, silent sentinels watching him arrive.

He sat in the car for a while, going over The Plan.

The Red Decree wanted him to die – so he could be born again.

So he could live again with his parents.

The same tragedy would repeat itself. He would lose them.

But this time, he would grieve.

He would cry.

Savannah had fallen for the temptation set by *The Red Decree*.

She cheated.

He never saw it happen – but the signs were there.

Red lips.

Late nights.

Distance.

The Red Decree knew that was the only thing that would set him off.

To kill his Savannah.

Not because he was a monster.

But because that was the price of rebirth.

The Red Decree wanted everything he'd ever loved erased.

So that when it finally took him too –

There'd be no one left to grieve.

Now, he had to finish it.

He would do it to himself.

They would find him eventually –

Shot in the head.

A gun in his hand.

Savannah on the passenger seat.

Together, they'd look like they were driving somewhere peaceful.

To paradise.

He didn't realise he was breathing too fast.

His chest rose and fell in quick, shallow bursts.

He caught his eyes in the rearview mirror.

A strange high flooded his body.

It was too much to bear.

He unfastened his seatbelt, swung the door open, and stepped out.

He looked behind him.

The township was still.

Faint sounds of dogs barking in the distance.

Insects singing in the shadows.

The air hung heavy with silence.

He moved quickly to the boot.

It clicked open with a soft pop.

He took a deep breath and lifted it fully – ready to move the body to the passenger seat.

But it was empty.

MAN OF THE HOUSE: AN ELDEST DAUGHTER'S STORY

DASHALIA SINGARAM

THE AIR WAS HEAVY but cooler after the afternoon storm – the one that had happened over the 'formerly' sleepy hollow – and the one that was ravaging through me. Still, my cheeks flamed hot and I felt like a supervillain as my anger steamed the air around me. I heard my mother shout my name in the distance but I was already floating away from the scene that was unfolding down the road at my childhood home. I saw the Uber pull up outside the complex gate and my legs ran clumsily and desperately for escape. I yanked at the door handle repeatedly before realising it was locked. The startled driver waved his hand up at me to pause. I pulled the door open, slipped myself through and closed it all in one swift motion. The new car smell surprised me, as did the friendliness of the driver.

Pietermaritzburg had become renowned since I'd escaped at the age of eighteen. First came the Ubers. Then the riots. For many South Africans, that was the first time they heard of the town. And first impressions live long past the tragedy that follows. Before that, there were stories of cannibalism, political assassinations and serial killers. Femicide ran rampant through the suburbs and the settlements. Just down the road from my mother's house, a man once beat his girlfriend to death and cut off her head. Domestic disputes had evolved into domestic terrorism and I had the startling realisation that I, too, was in danger of contributing to those statistics. The image of his body crumpled next to the bed made me shudder and I looked out of the steamy window for a sign of something, anything familiar. What if I had done it? What if I'd killed my own father?

I could think of nowhere to escape to in my long-forgotten hometown. 'The Mall'? With all the people? *I'd* rather die. The visceral reaction to what had just happened guided me to the safest place I could think of – the swings. The swings could fix anything. I directed the Uber driver across town, to a big plot of empty land near my dad's parents' house, where he still lived. If he still lived. I swallowed the thought like a big pill. Someone had the kindness years ago to erect a single set of swings right in the middle of the field. Nothing else, just that. It was home to one of the few memories I had with my dad, growing up. He came by every now and then and took me and whichever cousin was also housed at the shelter we knew as Amma's house to the swings. Sometimes the grass was long and we had to stomp through it to get there. But, once we were there, it was magic. I loved the swings. Being on them was the closest I ever felt to flying. And I longed to fly. Far away. Anywhere magical. My dad watched us, giving the occasional booster push until we had tired ourselves out. Palms bruised red from the metal chains and jeans covered in blackjacks all the way to the knees, we waded back out through the grass. That was then. When the Uber dropped me, I was shocked to discover the swings were no longer there. It was just an empty field now. I dropped defeated to my knees, cushioned by the thick long grass.

The argument had been building for two years, maybe longer. There had been only one other time that I remembered confronting my father. For a short man, he was an imposing figure in our house, absent but ever-looming. I hated him for most of my life. It grew slowly over the years, like a quiet cancer. The man was an absent alcoholic whose presence brought nothing but anger and pain. He walked into the house like he owned it, and 'parented' my siblings like he was one. My mother didn't help by pulling him back into our lives repeatedly because, 'At the end of the day, he's still your father.' By the time I was an adult, not only did I loathe him, but he could barely hide his disdain at my presence. He had never really cared for me at all, and his insistent 'parental' dominance was met with derision and a stubbornness on whose hill I was ready to die.

So, when he had a heart attack a few days ago and my mother called to let us know, I felt myself sinking into that all-too-familiar role of the eldest daughter. I booked a flight and went to take care of things. Of course, at the time I imagined … I don't know what I thought, really. We all thought he might die. It was his second dalliance with death in two years, and luck was not in our bloodline. My brother, my sister and I, by some miracle, happened to be together at my sister's place in Jo'burg when she got the call. My phone had been charging and the missed call was not forgotten by my mother, even in the stress of the moment. It was the first thing she mentioned when I met her in the hospital parking garage. Tensions had been high between the two of us since she declared that I was 'throwing my life away with drugs and alcohol, just like my father'. The statement was a knife in the gut and I've been struggling to pull it from my mind ever since.

Two years ago, I was sitting with my brother on the veranda of our mother's house. I was visiting for the weekend and he was almost at the end of his gap year. He sat taking hits off his bong as I dragged on my cigarette. It had been a stressful time and I had been smoking again for a few months. The old faithful crutch had never failed me. We were chatting, shit-talking, the ramblings of two traumatised, darkly hilarious kids, sharing bits and pieces of truth in the haze of the smoke around us. I looked at him as I ashed my cigarette over my mother's precious plants. 'I'm so happy,' I whispered to him, 'I'm scared something bad is going to happen.' He grinned the grin of someone who's truly happy for you, and I smirked. It really felt like everything was falling into place right then: the home, the boy, the job. After all the years of taking care of everyone else, it finally felt like it was my time.

Then, maybe a week after my whispered confession into the universe, my phone rang. It was my dad. He had called a few days before but I had missed the call. I meant to phone back. During the chaos of the pandemic and his newfound sobriety, we had been chatting. It was the closest thing to a relationship I'd ever had with him. As much as I hated to admit it, I didn't hate it. I answered the phone and an unfamiliar woman's voice greeted me. My stomach dropped. I knew something was wrong. It was the woman my dad had been seeing. He had been madly in love with her for almost a year. Until he heard that she was cheating on him with several patrons of the pub he owned.

He told me two weeks earlier when I found him drunk in the pub with two of his drinking buddies that I remembered from my childhood, now older and sadder. He was heartbroken. It took all the strength in me to hold back the anger, frustration and amusement at his situation. I had stopped by to drop off some food and sweetmeats from a family prayer gathering. My mom waited in the car while my brother accompanied me up the stairs to the all-too-familiar building that in all honesty had always been the love of my father's life.

I saw his yellowed eyes behind the bar and I stopped my brother in his tracks. 'Go wait for me in the car.' 'What? Why?' He was fourteen years younger than me but had become scarily protective as he reached adulthood. 'Just go. I'll be down soon,' I said in my no-nonsense voice. 'Are you sure?' he asked, his forehead creasing with worry. I nodded sternly and he reluctantly made his way back down the stairs. I turned to look at my father across the bar and gave him the same stern look. He walked over, a bleary smile on his face. Without saying a word, I walked him to the little alcove at the top of the stairs.

'How long?' I asked.

'Just today,' he replied. I rolled my eyes.

'Do you swear?'

'I swear.'

'Swear on your . . . no, *my* life?' I challenged.

'I swear on your life I have not been drinking.'

He explained how he was heartbroken over the loss of the woman in his life and had taken to the bottle just the night before. My head said wow, karma really is a bitch. But my heart, my heart was shattering as I looked at his swollen face, eyes glazed over. I couldn't believe we were back there again. As he started to cry I thought, people need other people, for times like these. I gave him the most impassioned, pleading speech of my life. He was my dad, after all. Pleading for him not to give up, reasoning that anything in life was possible. I mean, I was standing there. Who would have thought that would ever happen? I begged him, yes, begged him, to think about his family. His children. I begged for us to be enough. As I walked down those stairs to the car, I gathered the shattering pieces and swallowed them deeply.

The woman on the phone started speaking and her words washed over me without really sinking in. He had been missing for a few days. No one had seen or heard from him, so she went to look for him at his house and found him there. Barely conscious, with blood running down his head. The paramedics said it was a miracle he was still breathing. She'd been with him all day at the local government hospital waiting for him to be seen and needed a break to eat and shower. 'Is there *anyone* that can come?' I called my mom and begged her to please go and relieve the woman. She made me promise that she would not have to see her. I negotiated the situation from across the country and held my breath as I waited.

Later, I received a WhatsApp message from Mom. It was a video. In two seconds, I saw the remnants of a man I barely recognised, sitting in a wheelchair with a bandage hastily wrapped over his head. He looked homeless, haggard and drunker than I had ever seen in my life. I wondered for a second if I would die for the lie he had told me – *on your life* ringing through my head for hours and then days. I watched the video over and over again until I felt sick.

I found my mother near the hospital entrance. She smiled tearfully and greeted me warmly. I was shut down for survival and replied with a terse 'Hello'. I really didn't know what to expect; messages over the past few days hadbeen confusing and fraught with inconsistencies. In desperation, I called my dad's doctor friend – we called him 'Prof', a nickname he had acquired as the smart kid in school. He had been there at the last near-death encounter and would know what was really going on. In the meantime, I would go find out for myself. My brain had been recovering from burnout cycles for the past couple of years, and I dipped deep into the reserves for the mental strength I needed. By some miracle, we ran into the cardiac specialist on the way into the ward, a middle-aged Asian man with glasses and kind eyes. He hadn't been to see my dad in a couple of days and I was ready for shit to get done. In heavily accented English, he told me what had happened. 'Ahh yes! I know! Your father collapse in Casualty already. They see no pulse and they start with CPR. They do CPR for fifteen minutes but still nothing.'

'Fifteen minutes?' I asked. Every possible scenario flooded my head and I struggled to concentrate on what he was saying. 'Yes, fifteen minute. Then I walk past on my way to ward and see all crowded around him and I say no! Move move move! We pull the bed into the passage while they carry on CPR. Then we do the shock, I see nothing. We shock again, still nothing. Then, on fourth try we see he come back.' He carried on talking, explaining the procedures that had followed and the challenges to overcome. But, I had mentally removed myself from the room, from the hospital, from reality. Fifteen minutes. He was dead for fifteen minutes. And then a series of small miracles had colluded in the universe to somehow save him. 'Your father very lucky man. Very lucky.' The nurses behind him nodded in agreement. It was a miracle. I felt like I should be smiling but nothing stirred in my soul.

I moved like a zombie behind my mother towards his room, bracing myself for the sight of near death. We turned right into the room and saw an old man asleep in the first bed by the door. I exhaled and kept walking, turned the corner around the hospital curtain to be met with a scene I could never have expected. There was my dad. Without his backwards cap he actually looked like the 60-year-old that he was. His hair was greying and unkempt. Later, he told me he was trying to grow it out. Wisps of black and grey curls hung around his neck only to disappear past his ears. He was sitting up in the bed, not talking but chatting, with a huge smile across his face. I was speechless. My brain stuttered as it tried to reconcile what I was seeing with the information I had just been given. He saw me and his smile widened further. My body took over and I was beyond grateful for my survival instincts in that moment. I sat in that room and listened while he told his near-death story with the riveting passion of a Christ born again. I tried to share some careful adult advice and calm his ADHD with white lies and misdirection. In the end, I think we both frustrated each other to the point of both of us needing a smoke. And then we gave up, at least I did.

I left before visiting hours were over, letting my mother and some long-lost cousins fawn over 'the man that lived' and called Prof from the parking lot. I was fending off a panic attack that I could feel rising in my chest. I'd kill for a cigarette. He answered the phone after a few seconds and I explained the stress coursing through me. 'He's not taking this seriously. He thinks it's all some cool party trick. And he still doesn't have a hospital plan!'

'Don't worry, darling.' News of my mental break-down had travelled far and wide since the last time my father nearly died. 'I've taken care of everything for the hospital and I promise you, if this doesn't give him the wake-up call he needs, nothing will.' All I could think of was the old man in the bed telling his story like an excited kid who'd fallen off his bike during a wicked trick. Maybe nothing would change. He was discharged two days later and it was nothing short of miraculous. I obligingly went with my mother to fetch him from the hospital. The three of us hadn't spent that much time alone together since before my sister was born.

I had no idea how long I'd been sitting amongst the ghost of the swings and my sparse childhood but it was getting dark and a cold evening breeze blew the long grass around me. I had settled into a yogi-like position, facing the spot where the swings used to be. My knees creaked as I slowly pulled myself to my feet. For a second I wondered if he was already dead, but I shook the thought out of my head and started walking. I should get somewhere safe, I thought. But there were only a few familiar places in the area, all laced thick with trauma. I let my legs lead me while my brain drifted back to before. Before everything.

My father was a small man who lived in the centre of his own small world and rarely saw any perspective beyond his own. As a child it would infuriate me, but over the years I'd learnt to tune out his narcissism like white noise.

It truly wasn't personal. It was always about him. I walked up the road and my feet turned the corner before I realised. It was my dad's street. I recognised his car parked in the road before anything. Some of the houses looked the same, and his house cast that same foreboding shadow onto the street below that I remembered as a kid. His car being there meant he had driven it there himself. So that meant . . . he was alive! Relief washed away the thought of prison cells and a life crippled by guilt. And then, fear filled its place. Fear that this would never be over.

The discharge from hospital had been a slow and painful process, the most brutal test of my patience in a long time. I could feel my patience waning at the second, and then third recounting of his narrow escape from mere mortality. He had been chatting with more people in the hospital and now had perspectives and colour for the tale. I gritted my teeth but eventually a few snide remarks escaped my lips. All disguised as jokes, of course. I'm not the devil. The man had just died. The two bong hits I'd had before going to the hospital certainly hadn't hurt. As he chatted away while my mother wheeled him to her car, I interjected. 'So basically, you're saying you got kicked out of hell?' My loud and obnoxious laugh echoed through the near empty parking lot and then reverberated in my chest. I bit my lip, knowing it was anger spilling out of me, but I would die before I apologised to him.

In all my years, every shitty and painful interaction I'd had and not had with my father – not once had he ever apologised. When the kids in school asked me who the women picking me up after school were – was that my mom? No, she works for my dad. Not technically a lie but a blackened truth instead. I was ashamed of our life. There were so many affairs, way more than I could remember. At some point, every couple of months my mother would come into the room in angry tears. I didn't ask questions. I knew what needed to be done. I began packing my sister's clothes and baby things into the mint green bucket we used to fill her baby bath. I'd pack some clothes and my school things and then we would be off. She was leaving his drinking, cheating ass. We were moving back to Amma's safe house. But, as these stories often go, time would pass, he would come pleading, *swearing* 'ne-ver again' and off we went, mint green bucket and my growing anxiety in tow. Three years went by that way. The chaos at home became normal. I began to lie at school, knowing that it wasn't normal but not having any idea what was. I couldn't understand it, couldn't understand why we kept going back. My mother would vent all her frustrations to me and I would listen keenly, searching for solutions. I knew what adultery was before I knew what sex was. No one had ever apologised for that.

So, he had survived the argument. An argument that had brewed for years and exploded at the worst possible moment. We had left the hospital and driven to my mom's house where she'd set up my brother's old room for the man to recover in. I was running on empty and dying to get out of that house and out of that town. I helped carry his bags in and, the three of us huddled in the small room, I said, 'So, shall we talk?' After one of my snarky comments at the hospital, he had eventually had enough and said, sternly, 'We'll talk about that later.' There was a tinge of fear, but the anger and resentment at the two people who stood before me had taken over. I wasn't the scared peacekeeper anymore, not the broken telephone, not the makeshift parent of their other children, or of them. My mother had been fighting it, the decline and fall of the make-believe empire I had built over the years. Held together with staples, old chewing gum and many, many lies behind walls. It was pretty impressive from the outside and had held against all odds for the better part of thirty years.

But I was done. I had broken, burnt out, thrown my life away as they say. But little did I know, I wasn't the only one who had been dying to have their say. 'What?! What do you need to say to me, huh?' The testimonial that followed felt prepared and targeted. A barrage of complaints, snide insults and character assassinations flowed like fresh lava from his lips. I could sense the fear as my mother tensed in the doorway. But, I wasn't the reliable eldest daughter anymore. I was not there to make everything better while shoving my feelings down my own gagging throat. In that moment, I was done.

'You wanna know why I'm like this?'

'Oh, don't tell me. It's just who you are?' he retorted.

'No. No. It's so far from who I am! But you, you bring out the most hateful part of me!' He came at me with the whole 'who do you think you are, if you were a man do you know what I would do' schpiel. I looked the small man directly in the eyes and took a step towards him. 'Well? Here I am.' My hands were trembling, but I stood fast.

My mother squeezed herself between us, using her arms to create a safety barrier. Of course I wasn't going to hit a recently dead man, but I wasn't going to walk away either. I looked at my mother, seething, and said, 'Don't you ever, ever compare me to this man again!' I stepped back from them both and, with narrowed eyes and a steadied voice, said, 'I am one hundred times the man you will ever be! I could be cracked out in a ditch in the street and still, still I would be better than you. I always have been.' As I turned to leave the room, I saw him stumble and try to steady himself with a hand on the bed. Pause filled the room, and the next few seconds moved like lava, each moment slowly rolling over to the next. His hand slipped and he managed to grab hold of the covers. He stood defiantly and looked me straight in the eyes. His gaze held me in my step like a spell. And then slowly, piece by piece, he started to fall. Each joint bent and collapsed against one another before he met the carpet. His eyes fluttered and then, all at once, time and noise and reality returned to the room. 'Sevaaaaa!!!! Seva!! What have you done?!' My mother shrieked as she bent down to his bundled body. 'I . . . I . . . ' I raced out of the room, out the front door and up the road.

Standing outside his house now, I wasn't sure what I was feeling. Yes, there was relief. But there was something else. As I tried to figure out what it was, the front door opened. Alive and in the flesh, my father stepped out onto the veranda with a cigarette between his lips. He lifted a lighter to it and, as he did, our gazes met. I was grateful for the distance between us. It was needed. It had always been there. From the moment that 13-year-old me had ripped my brother's tiny wrist from his grip, before his other hand came crashing down to hit him. Right then, when I scooped him up to what I hoped was safety, our eyes met with the same look. Defiance met with disdain. I took a second to breathe out the pain of that memory, then turned and walked down the street without looking back. He didn't come after me I knew he wouldn't.

AFRICAN DEATH, WESTERN MEDICINE

LETHUKUKHANYA MZULWINI

'I DO.' THESE WORDS carried so much promise when Bhekizizwe and I exchanged our vows all those years ago. Today, all I have left to boast about to the women's league at church is the precious stone on my finger.

Cleaning my husband's study, I remove the ring to avoid dust getting on it. My absence from our house over the past four weeks has meant that the furniture and cabinets have grown dusty and grimy. As I wipe the cupboards I find – tucked against my fine China dinnerware and Bhekizizwe's theology certificates – our wedding album. I trace my finger lightly along the golden cursive embroidery stitched into the fabric which reads, 'Bhekizizwe weds Thandaza'. An inscription on the book's jacket professes, 'Where there is love, there's no darkness'. After ten years of marriage, this proverb no longer holds the same hope it did back then. It seems my husband is only capable of loving me in the darkness. In the light of day, *imina isinyama*, (he sees me as a dark cloud).

My children possess no names. Bhekizizwe forbade me from naming them. He says the act of naming a child is a prayer. With the powers bestowed upon him, he only prays over the living. He says naming unborn children would be acknowledging their existence as ghosts that will contaminate our home. Four weeks ago, before I left home, I overheard him tell the church elders that my attachment to the babies we've lost is a trauma response. 'My wife's obsession with these spirits is rooted in pain,' he said. 'God will get us through it all.' Perhaps I haven't come to terms with the losses. Perhaps this is why I often hear their crying resounding in my mind, ringing through the passageways of our home.

Dr Abdullahi and the nurses at the hospital have spent the last four weeks trying to help rid me of these visions and the terrible headaches that accompany them. For weeks the medication numbed me as I drifted aimlessly from one group therapy session to another. Introductions to patients who, like me, seemed to be shells of their former selves. During my stay in the hospital, we were all disconnected from the outside world. No mobile devices, no television. The only threads we had connecting us to our previous lives came in the form of our loved ones who arrived on Sunday afternoons to share a meal with us in the dining hall.

I'd sit for most of the visiting hours hoping Bhekizizwe would show up earlier than he had in the previous week. Dr Abdullahi would encourage the nurses to make me eat, but I always insisted on waiting for my husband to join me first. Over the month I spent in that hospital, Bhekizizwe showed up in uniform fashion, only ever arriving for the last ten minutes of our visit. I'd hear him speaking to Dr Abdullahi in hushed tones, greeting the nurses in the corridor before praying over all of us. He never once uttered a word directly to me, refused to ever let his gaze meet mine. Instead, he'd lay his hands on my head, his touch growing colder by the week. He'd speak in tongues, rebuking my sickness, purging me of my demons, silencing their voices. The last time we had spoken of these voices was when he had first dropped me off at the psychiatric hospital. Before that, I'd gone to consult with Gogo Nomvula, an *isangoma* who had warned me that these voices I kept hearing were the result of *amanono*, spirits of unnamed departed babies.

Bhekizizwe was furious when I told him that I'd been consulting Gogo; that's what finally pushed him to get me admitted into the facility. When I tried to explain what Gogo had told me, he refused to listen, blaming the voices on demonic possession. At first, he ordered the church elders to visit me at our home. After hearing the rumours that had spread through our community that *'umam'fundisi useyahlanya'* (the preacher's wife has gone mad) they arrived bearing hymns and prayers. When these prayers failed to deter the voices, the congregants assisted my husband in covering my hospital expenses, with the psychiatrists adding another reading to my diagnosis. Dr Abdullahi had claimed that what I was suffering from was not demonic possession, nor was it an ancestral calling but a medical condition known as schizophrenia.

I was discharged yesterday with a prescription of pills I was told will quieten the voices and quell my headaches. I returned home the night before my husband's Sunday service and lay snuggled on my side of the bed while Bhekizizwe spent most of the night in his study, preparing his sermon. I woke up later than usual on Sunday morning. Dr Abdullahi did warn us that the side effects of the medication would cause some drowsiness and fatigue.

Upon waking, I catch a whiff of freshly ground coffee beans and spices coming from the kitchen and the sound of butter and bacon fat simmering in the frying pan, alongside a gentle humming. Bhekizizwe is still in the shower. I rise steadily from the bed and make my way to the kitchen to investigate who is there.

She turns before I can utter a word, feeling my presence as I observe her. It's Phindile, daughter of MaNdlovu. MaNdlovu is one of the leading members of the women's league at the church. Her daughter is a sweet young child whom I remember from the worship team. My rocky relationship with MaNdlovu makes me uneasy about seeing Phindile standing there in my kitchen, wearing my apron.

Phindile sheepishly greets me, 'Saw'bona Mam'fundisi, I hope I didn't wake you with my singing?'

'Phindile, what are you doing here?' I ask.

'I thought you were still away, Mama. I was instructed by church elders to come and assist Bab' Bhekizizwe with domestic chores while you were recovering in hospital.'

Phindile utters these words while fumbling to untie the knots of my apron. She slips off the apron and hands it to me somewhat apologetically.

'Go get ready for church, child,' I say. By the time I finish the sentence she's already vanished out the kitchen door.

I take the reins in the kitchen, dish up breakfast and proceed to iron Bhekizizwe's vestment. What are MaNdlovu and those church elders up to, I wonder. Are they trying to replace me with this young woman? Her presence in my house felt like a threat, a plot that had been carefully orchestrated in my absence. I made an oath *ngehlobo leminyaka eyishumi edlule* (in the summer of 2015), not only to my husband, but to the whole church. 'I shall not damage the purity of my husband. I shall be a good wife.' That is all I have ever tried to be to him.

When we get back from church in the afternoon, I labour tirelessly in the kitchen – chopping, slicing and dicing, honouring the ring on my finger. When I serve Bhekizizwe his meal, he cannot bring himself to look at me. His gravy stays untouched. The steamed bread loses all steam. Kitchen knives might as well cut the tension in the room, for they serve no purpose as cutlery. The silence across our dinner table is as loud as the wrath of my ancestors. I am the burning bridge between an outraged ancestry and its descendants suffocating inside me. Infants I bear never see the light of day. Bhekizizwe can't resist holding God liable for every futile foetus we are left to mourn. I watched him up on that pulpit today, with a crooked smile on my face, the same rehearsed smile I've worn for the last ten years. He plays God's advocate so well. I witness the transition every Sunday. Like today, for instance, he let out the words, 'God's servants endure the most severe storms.' The congregation stood in unison shouting 'hallelujah!' and 'amen!' whilst scraping for the last bits of loose change from their purses to add to the collection plates.

Bhekizizwe's verbosity and voice have not followed him home from the pulpit. He sits silently, not touching his meal. Some nights he bangs the table, raging against God or me for the miscarriages, a tug of war for who gets the blame. This evening, his bitterness is steeped in silence. Silence for the infants conceived but never born within our marriage. Our home is colder and more haunted than the ghost town residing within my womb. Parts of me keep dying with every miscarriage. My body has become a hollow shell, a vessel previously occupied by my husband's once dutiful and joyful wife.

I strip naked on the nights that nature comes knocking. In the name of fulfilling my wifely duties, I let him host a search party inside me. Heavy breaths scented with communion wine conjure a trail of goosebumps from my neck right down to my navel as they tell the good lie, 'Bhekizizwe still loves me'. I fall for it every time. He digs deeper, devouring me with the carnal intensity that leaves my drenched walls convulsing as he hunts for parts of me that have gone missing. My husband is a necrophiliac. The candles snuffed out at dusk, I let him mingle with my ghost. When the sun comes up, he once more sees me as the devil roaming around the lounge. I listen to the stereo with the sound off, hoping his voice will fill the void. The blank television set stares back into my wretched eyes.

I have been carrying daggers in my heart ever since *ubizo lami*, my calling. uMamezala, my mother-in-law, continues feeding her son the rotten broth of judgement. I hear her whisper conspiratorially to him in the other room after she has sent me away to wash the dishes.

'This village bears so many fruits, Bhekizizwe. Beautiful fruits like Phindile. You should consider *isthembu*, polygamy. Taking a second wife like your father wouldn't be such a bad idea. Your wife is not Sarah from the Bible. God helps those who help themselves. Are you really prepared to surrender your father's bloodline to *isinyama salentombazane* – the curse of this girl?'

uMamezala's provocation hangs in the room before Bhekizizwe responds in an impatient whisper. 'I'm working on it, Ma,' he says, thinking I cannot hear him. His words have consequences, more so than the words of uMamezala who calls the gifts bestowed upon me *isinyama*. More so than the congregation who whisper to each other in the tea garden after the service, 'Bhekizizwe's wife is cursed, that's why she can't conceive. That's why she's in and out of the mental asylum.'

But how can I be cursed when my ancestors say I'm blessed? Ever since I've been summoned by them, Bhekizizwe and I have become strangers. *Ubizo*, the calling, chases me in my sleep. Night sweats wash over me as their voices rise like a tide, plunging me into the deep end with the promise that I will be regurgitated safely back onto the shore if I surrender to their call. My deceased grandmother, Gogo Zibuyile, is the lifeguard. She offers a helping hand every night. '*Sabela uyabizwa*. You are chosen, Thandaza. *Ungokhethiwe*,' she utters sternly whilst coming to the rescue of my engulfed soul. I wake and kneel beside the bed, rebuking my ancestors in the name of Jesus Christ, reminding myself that I am the preacher's wife and that I must not falter, I must wear my title with pride. I must not confide in anyone but our Lord.

I return to consult with Gogo Nomvula again in secret. 'You are drowning in denial,' she tells me. 'It is your religious beliefs that are keeping you from accepting the truth.' I leave my shoes at the door that leads into her shrine, a shrine sanctified with totems, indigenous textiles and animal skin ornaments that hang from her shelves.

Gogo always likes to remind me, 'It is here that one's soul comes for surgery.' Upon taking my seat on the reed mat, I see Gogo Nomvula's grim expression through the clouds of *impepho* smoke. As the dried ancestral herb smoulders and hangs thick in the air, my spirit begins to stir. Gogo Nomvula puffs some air into her bag, throws down her bones and offers me a diagnosis.

She is the conduit to my ancestors and, through her, they speak to me. 'Thandaza, what sickness brings you to *umsamu* today?' Gogo Nomvula's question travels from behind the cloud of incense. I offer a predictable response, 'I need to strengthen my marriage, Gogo.'

Without regarding my plea, she asks me curiously, '*Kunjani*, Thandaza? How are you?'

I struggle to hold back my tears. 'I'm hurting. Bhekizizwe is considering taking a second wife. I'm certain it's his mother who's behind all this chaos.'

'I suppose the bishop is still not taking well to your calling,' Gogo Nomvula says. 'Strengthening your marriage at this point *ukuthela amanzi emhlane wedada* – it's as vain as pouring water down a duck's back. Temporary solutions have already proven to you that you are spiralling further and further into a spiritual dilemma. You have refused to be obedient to the call of your elders. Many who came before you from your bloodline have done the same. The sins of your forebears have fallen upon you.'

Feeling my sorrow turning to fury, I cry out. 'Why am I the scapegoat for their transgressions, Gogo? I never asked for any of this. The miscarriages. How can my own blood be so cruel as to place these tragic burdens upon me?'

'Make no mistake, your elders want what's best for you, Thandaza. These burdens are gifts you are refusing to embrace. You are the compass to direct your lineage towards greater prosperity.' Gogo responds calmly.

Distraught, I reply, 'I am being sacrificed for a system I do not believe in. What will the church say? Bhekizizwe and I do not practise these beliefs. Accepting them will only drive me further from my husband and my community, and further into loneliness. They will only prescribe me more and more medicine to stop this madness.'

'You are only running away from yourself, Thandaza. The spiritual warfare to which you're exposing these children is bigger than you think. You've been called to be the healer for a generation of thorned spirits. No amount of Western medicine will ever be enough to stop these African deaths. I am aware of the measures you have taken to find alternative cures, exorcisms to wash off what is essentially written in your DNA. Do you wish for a bloodline of walking dead souls to come through your womb? These generational curses demand to be broken at some point, either by you or the children you so desperately yearn for, to strengthen your marriage. But I must warn you that even when you lean into these more temporary solutions, your offspring will continue to be cast into limbo, disoriented souls stuck in a chasm destructive to their spiritual well-being. Maybe then your eyes will be opened to the fact that paying no heed to your ancestors' call has repercussions. Your refusal to heed their words will continue to wreak terrible consequences.'

Her final words are a parting gift worthy of thinking about as I return home. When I get home in the evening, I heat up the stove. Gogo Nomvula's words linger in my mind. I tie my apron and cement myself at the kitchen counter for a final time, chopping, slicing and dicing.

At dinner with Bhekizizwe, he sits staring vacantly at the plate of food I've placed in front of him. His gravy remains untouched. Once again, the steamed bread loses its steam. I unpack the bottles of pills I was given by Dr Abdullahi and lay them on the dinner table before him. Next to them, I place my Women's Ministry leadership badge. Bhekizizwe's eyes lift ever so slightly, but still he says nothing.

I slide the ring off my finger and place it resolutely beside the other items. It taps the wood of the table gently.

I do.

In this tug of war between oblivion and truth, I choose peace.

. . . I do.

LETTERS OF REMEMBRANCE
SEBABATSO MADIBU

21/05/2087

Hi Papa.

I must write everything down.

The way your sleeves trembled as you coughed.

Deep. Evading the cancer in your lungs.

I must see it. Again and again.

You said it's part of the conversion –

Before I left.

You called it neural integration.

A surgical phase that bends the past out of shape.

So we forget the kind of joy they can't sell back to us.

We forget that the sun shines without asking for anything.

Laminating Berea in native light.

In Sandton, the sun doesn't shine like the one back home.

Instead it stares; without promise.

Like the mystery of our existence.

'Please, my child,' Mama said.

'Just go build a better life.'

Those were her last words to me.

Before she gave in beneath the washing line.

Her body, a shadow of duty. Of robbed decisions.

Destiny weaved by the cyborgs.

The ones who don't hire the broken.

The ones who have no use for brittle lungs.

For men like Papa; and women like Mama.

For those who are too human to convert.

30/05/2087

Hi Papa,

'Lie still. Relax,' says the nurse,

unfolding my body onto the stretcher.

Beside me, glints a tray of tools –

Standard for civilian-grade chrome.

And there are different kinds of chrome.

Military-grade. Domestic.

Every lung, every part –

Either patented, taxed or owned.

This is the sale of survival

Bought for me by my mother's brother

Uncle Jeff – a story she told about climbing – not just out of flesh, but into dignity.

His daughter, Sine, who once called me her sister.

We are bonded by the knowledge of motherless life.

Now chrome life – far from dry taps and power cuts.

From the rebels back home.

Who fight not from anger

But because they remember

They remember a world where breathing didn't cost you your body.

Maybe even your soul.

'Please sit up,' the nurse commands, pausing just long enough to pretend it's a choice.

I rise, denting my elbows into the threadbare sheet. Her eyes scan my vitals.

'Will I lose my memories?'

Her gaze meets mine; holding back, warning. Something like concern.

'The transition is a phased process,' she replies, now holding a syringe. 'This is so that your body does not reject the chrome.'

'But my memo –

'Can you please confirm your guardian to me?' Her voice, a nudge of wisdom to let it go.

Offering my arm, I whisper, 'It's okay.'

To the nurse. To the stretcher.

'It will all be okay.'

08/06/2087

Hi Papa,

'Everyone in the dining room in five minutes!'

Uncle Jeff yells, his voice cutting from the hall downstairs.

'Already?' Sine remarks, as she slips on her sync gloves.

I reach for mine, but my fingers retract with each stretch.

'Can you cover for me?' I plead, now reaching for Mama's cloth.

Red and white, dusted with snuff.

Black and yellow, spelling Ntsu.

'You can't be serious,' she says, as if looking too long might make her stupid.

On Tuesdays, we sit for data syncs – me, Sine, and Uncle Jeff.

Palms to the console, as our memories are sieved:

pertinent / non-pertinent.

It's like praying without a priest.

'Fine,' she exhales, putting on the second glove. 'But hurry.'

The door slams shut like a command as I unfold the cloth now covering a section of my bed.

My makeshift shrine.

'Where's Nandi?' I hear Uncle Jeff say.

As I wrap my hands with Mama's rosary.

As I kneel before the bed.

I have to remember.

'Nandi?' his voice cracks.

Like the crackle of the vinyl that sang Mama's soul.

Letta Mbulu's voice: *There's music in the air.*

Even now, as it exhales old wounds.

The hallway creaks.

Each step heavier than the last.

Like the last words Papa said to me.

'Nandi?' Uncle Jeff calls –

Disrupting the recall of Papa's cigarette.

Smoke curling like a dancing curtain.

And then a sigh breaks into the violent wind tearing through the room.

'I just need two minutes,' I whisper, jaw clenched with will.

But he edges forward.

'Let's go,' Uncle Jeff finally says.

His knee looming by my face.

But I keep my gaze low.

My head still bowed.

In vow to memory.

14/06/2087

Hi Papa,

To mark my new sight,

Uncle Jeff took me and Sine to the Preserve.

'The garden of origin,' they call it.

Of living people, living things. Soon to be bones in the soil.

'Those lilies … ' he exclaims, his hands wide on the steering wheel. As if the flower itself were beauty's testimony.

Then softer, he whispers:

'Your mother would've liked them.'

Like a promise I would too.

The car continues forward.

Until on the dash: a shaky clip blinks.

Snapping even Sine from half-sleep.

It is Berea's gravesite.

Burning.

'Butt is not the cyborgs,' the news voice states. Almost even.

'But a new, confirmed human rebel group called Abogata.'

'Papa,' I answer, like instinct.

And yet, Uncle Jeff is still staring.

Now in righteous disgust.

As if he doesn't understand the cause.

Of law bleeding to dust.

At the bottom of a beer.

In the curve of someone's hip.

Arched, like the gate of the Preserve.

Which unfurls in perfect hue.

Slow and deliberate

A voice on the intercom greets us:

'Forty Africoins per unit. Please confirm chrome grade.'

Past the gates, the gravel looks swept by hand.

The benches gleam like they've never been sat on.

And the flowers.

They don't bloom.

They present themselves.

Each one glistening in symmetrical obedience.

'That's the white jewel,' Uncle Jeff says.

Pointing to the bed of lilies centring the room.

Our steps whisper around the vase;

cyborgs tracing petals like curators.

'Tell me you see it?' he asks.

Now resting his hand on my shoulder.

It wasn't until the shrubs shivered in the manufac-
tured wind

Until a rose glinted like a diamond.

I finally understood.

We're not in a garden.

We're in a zoo.

01/07/2087

Dear Papa,

'If I had a cigarette for every pothole,'

You'd laugh, strike a match.

Resting on the camp chair overlooking the ones on our street.

When it rained, the potholes filled.

Like little mirrors.

Little lakes.

Ke mang, ke mang, ke mang?

Ke mang ya ka fuduwang letsha lena?

Mama singing as she hangs the washing.

My hands, shifting pebbles at your feet.

'What does that mean?' I ask, tracing circles in the dirt.

A rough rasp rattles your reply, 'Who can stir this lake?'

'Stir this lake?'

'Yes, like your mother stirs a pot.'

Still caught in wonder, I whisper, 'A lake?'

'Only God, Nandipha. Only God's great big hand can stir a lake.'

I imagine it slicing through the white light above,

the one that stares down like the Sandton sun.

Naked beneath the surgical gown. Arms strapped. Chin cupped by a foam brace.

Phase 3 is coming.

I can already smell the antiseptic

The acute click of joints being locked and unlocked.

Motor calibration

It is the step before neural integration

Where they'll finally sync my memories to the chrome.

So tonight, I hold it all a little closer.

Like a piece of hidden toffee,

Bitten piece by piece.

03/07/2087

Dear Papa,

They say you died.

Not from the cyborgs' raid.

Not in the rebels' riot.

But the air. Dirty human air.

The one littered by the cyborgs.

'Your father would want you to be strong,' Uncle Jeff says.

Hovering behind my back.

'Be strong like your mother.'

That's when I take off.

My breath catching before my feet.

Past neighbouring houses blinking the same green light.

Past silver fences, I graze my knees against the stone.

Before I shelter behind a broken wall, switching off my locator.

The wind: cold, stinging.

Against the last patch of skin they haven't plated.

And yet the final phase is waiting;

'Don't come back,' you said to me,

as I left for Uncle Jeff's.

'Remember what your mother said.'

Stinging sharp. Something stinging.

'Nandi!'

Uncle Jeff calls.

Curt and commanding.

But the name falls short.

Missing syllable. Missing weight.

I shrink further away into the dark end of the wall,

imagining a yellow road leading me back home;

To the place where my name was whole. Nandipha.

Ringing.

Scolding in my head.

Like a lullaby folded with care.

'Nandi,' Uncle Jeff calls again.

This time a single light catches on my chrome.

'How many times?' he asks,

His boot crunching closer on the gravel.

'Nandi, get out!'

'No Uncle Jeff!' I retort – too fast, too loud.

Then softer. Spilling: 'Sorry.'

But he snaps, shouting, 'No,' like he's found the bruise and presses in. 'Phela you must say if you want to sleep outside tonight. You must say, if what you want, is to be treated like a dog. Or even worse,' pausing, 'like a human.'

'That's fine,' I resign, letting the night hold me.

But a sigh breaks, like a draft shivering.

'Nandi, I made promises to your mother.'

'But Papa's dead now,' I'm cracking, opening, like a pod split in two. 'Who's going to remind me?'

Breath still uneven, he asks 'Of what?'

'Please,' I beg, now pulling away from the dark end of the wall, 'I just need a minute.'

21/07/2087

Hi Papa,

This morning, I woke up facing east.

As if waiting for the sunrise.

Tomorrow is when I will begin the final phase.

The one that integrates memory.

Into chrome. Into silver promise.

I think I should eat.

So I can remember the last taste of hunger,

Eager; driving.

I still think of the nurse; her eye piercing my futile curiosity.

Now I know: my soul will die in that surgery.

In metal's crystalline structure;

My heart will melt into the maze of atoms

And there will be no ache

For any memory.

Captured in the press of your fingers.

Mama's voice in the next room.

Calling.

Not calling.

I have to forget.

That there was ever music in the air.

That there were poets in my mind.

Telling me stories about how Things Fall Apart.

In riot, in burning graves.

In empty taps. In black arid land.

But I see it still, the sun-lit road leading me back home.

Where the soil was thick from teary clouds.

Where the spinach bends with each rain drop.

Nodding. Whispering.

It is saying something.

It is saying, 'Something is coming.'

In these pages.

Memory will cling –

It will bloom.

Even when the wood from the tree is long pressed into paper.

Memory, like ink –

Will seep, sink and stain.

CONTRIBUTORS

Jacqui Aires has degrees in English and psychology, an MA in writing, and additional qualifications spanning her varied interests. Her passions include labour law, social justice and education. Jacqui is a veteran English teacher with a love for writing in all genres. She cofounded Write Jozi and lives in Johannesburg with her partner.

Megan Choritz is a writer, theatre maker, actor and improviser, living in Cape Town with her dog Frieda, her cat Jonesie and a cockroach hotel in her compost heap. She won praise for her debut novel *Lost Property* published in 2023.

Dyondzo Kwinika writes from South Africa's historically segregated communities, exploring identity, mental health and generational trauma. His work examines how history and culture shape the ways we love, grieve and change.

Sebabatso Madibu is a Johannesburg-based writer whose work explores the South African experience through new and imaginative forms. Her storytelling bridges past and present to imagine futures that interrogate what we inherit and how it moulds who we become. She is driven by the belief that South Africa's layered histories offer a wealth of untapped characters, contradictions and truths still waiting to be explored.

Lerato Mahlangu is short story writer from eMalahleni, Mpumalanga. Her short stories appear in anthologies including *One Life*, edited by Joanne Hitchens and Karina Szczurek. She was overall winner of the 2024 My World, My Words children's story writing competition – her story can be found in the *Mandla's Mark and Other Stories* anthology.

Kamva Majo is a South African writer whose story 'We Cannot Afford To Be Silent' was included in the *Power: Short.Sharp.Stories* anthology, edited by Joanne Hitchens. Her writing explores mental health, death and unsettling social realities. She hopes to continue blending realism with psychological horror in future work.

Lethukukhanya Mzulwini was born and bred in and has been inspired by Esikhawini, a small township in KwaZulu-Natal. He is drawn to the power of historical fiction and ancestral narratives, where the past informs the present and illuminates the future. His work explores the intricate threads of lineage and heritage, seeking answers to timeless questions and sparking new perspectives. Through storytelling, he aims to bridge the gaps between generations, cultures and experiences as well as uncover the hidden truths that shape our understanding of ourselves and the world around us.

Princess Unarine Rabada is a writer of stories and songs and a theatre practitioner from Limpopo. Her work is deeply inspired by her Venda roots, weaving themes of ancestral memory, womanhood and African spirituality into lyrical, emotionally rich narratives. She is passionate about preserving oral traditions through modern storytelling. Princess is currently working on new short fiction and continues to explore the intersections of culture, language and healing through her art.

Rosieda Shabodien is an executive coach, gender and development specialist, and writer whose creative non-fiction draws from her experiences growing up under apartheid. Her stories are love letters to resistance, steeped in history, longing, humour and the urgent act of remembering.

Dashalia Singaram is an engineer, a fixer and recovering people-pleaser, and a writer. She is on sabbatical (turned gap year) and finds herself flailing about in the same existential crises as many of her millennial peers, on a search for something more, something meaningful.